# EMMY IN HARDING

SAMANTHA ADKINS

Published in the United States by Wolfpack Publishing, Las Vegas

CKN Christian Publishing
An Imprint of Wolfpack Publishing
6032 Wheat Penny Avenue
Las Vegas, NV 89122

christiankindlenews.com

Paperback ISBN: 978-1-64119-982-7
eBook ISBN: 978-1-64119-981-0

# EMMY IN HARDING

# ACKNOWLEDGMENTS

With thanks to my late grandpa, A.L. Karras for his detailed book, North to Cree Lake: The Rugged Lives of the Trappers. I paraphrased several of his stories in this novel. I highly recommend this fascinating record of a lost way of life.

# AUGUST 1939

# CHAPTER ONE

*Summer Camp*

Living at home at eighteen was like wearing clothes that were too tight. Emmy Bennett loved her siblings and mother, but she was constantly suppressing frustration. In August of 1939, there were few options for a woman to escape her family home that didn't involve marriage. She couldn't wait for her camp counsellor position to begin.

There would be no remuneration for her work, but her food and transportation were provided for and she would have two weeks in the open air before she started teaching.

Twelve young people from the Shelby United Church piled into two old Model T's loaded with canvas tents, sleeping rolls, clothes and food and headed onto the prairie road. It was Emmy's first time at camp.

"Isn't this the life?" shouted her friend Bev over the roar of the open window. Bev's blond curls blew in the wind, tangling into more confusion with each passing mile. They'd both started with scarves, but Bev's had blown away only fifteen minutes into their trip. Emmy's remained firmly in place and her dark glossy hair didn't dare put on the wild, disorderly display that Bev's had.

Hot sun mixed with the dry dust of another drought-filled summer to parch the lips of the campers. Emmy and Bev sat in the back of one car with Catherine and Trudy while four boys sat in front. The boys passed a canteen between them, but the girls refused their offers to share. Their minister had given them strong warnings about acting as godly men and women during their week away. Hand holding and all other forms of affection would send a camper straight home in disgrace. Emmy figured sharing pressing their lips to a communal container could be seen as intimacy and had instructed the girls not to give into the temptation, but her determination wavered as the sun beat down on her dark head.

Emmy should never have worried about Catherine and Trudy. At seventeen, they already behaved like confirmed spinsters. Leaving home was outside of their imaginations.

"Won't it be terrible to live with strangers?" Catherine said. She'd been asking Bev and Emmy questions about teaching since leaving the church in Shelby. Emmy thought she should have started thinking of teaching earlier in the spring. All the best positions were taken.

"I'm sure they'll soon become like family," Bev

said. She was taller and thicker than Emmy. She had a perpetually warm smile and a way of making everyone she met feel like family.

"I think I'd be awfully homesick," said Trudy. Despite the heat and wind, Trudy wore a high collar and held her headscarf in place. "I'm already homesick and we're only going for two weeks."

Catherine hugged her friend. They were a striking pair – Trudy tall and severe, Catherine dark-haired and sprightly. They'd been friends since they met on the first day of school. "It'll be good for us," Catherine said.

"What would I do if you went off to teach and left me alone in Shelby?" Trudy shook her head.

"You'd come with me to cook and clean in the teacherage. You'd like that, wouldn't you Trude? Then I wouldn't have to live with strangers at all." Catherine smiled at her plan.

Trudy furrowed her brow and didn't speak again for an hour. She was the kind of girl who needed time to think.

They reached the lake before lunch and split into groups to attack different jobs. Most of the boys converged around the tent materials and grew more and more heated over the best way to place and raise the canvas. Emmy and Bev searched for water and wood. They had sandwiches for lunch but would need a bonfire to boil water and make supper. Catherine and Trudy continued their discussion of a teacherage as they spread out picnic blankets and prepared the lunch.

"Hello the camp!" Emmy turned to find a dark-haired young man in blue jeans, white collared shirt and a leather jacket striding toward them. He was not what she expected their theologian to look like.

"I'm Bill," he held out his hand.

Emmy was closest. She wiped her hand on her dress before taking his. "Emmy."

"You're the female counsellor," Bill put his hands on his hips and surveyed the effort. "How are things coming along?"

Emmy heard one of the boys curse from inside the canvas tent and flinched. "We're having a little trouble with the tents.

Bill lifted his chin. "Yep, they can be real buggers."

Emmy was surprised at his language but felt an ounce of comfort that their trained minister might not be as much of a stick as she'd expected.

He left to oversee the tents and soon she heard laughter and good-natured ribbing instead of quarrelling and swearing from the young men.

They had tea ready and everything in order once the tents were up.

"I could eat a horse," said Hap, the shortest of the teenagers. Beneath his suspenders, his white t-shirt was stained with dirt and sweat.

Bill prayed for the meal. "God, we thank Thee for gathering this group here in your beautiful creation. Bless this food to our bodies and bless our time together. Keep us from temptation and sin. Amen."

Emmy saw Charles and Jake exchange a look

after the prayer. They were not regular church-go-ers and she thought they must think Bill a goodie-two-shoes, but they didn't say anything. Soon their mouths were full of tea and sandwiches as they leaned back on the picnic blanket and their eyes drooped while they gazed at the sleepy lake before them.

Their make-shift camp sat amongst the Cotton-wood trees up from Lake Katepwa. The wide lake was set in the Qu'Appelle Valley, an anomaly in the endless flat prairies. The water beckoned to them as it lapped the sandy shore. Once they had rested a while, they put on their swim suits and rushed into the cool water.

Catherine and Trudy giggled and stole glances at the young men who dunked one another and took turns showing off their ability to skip rocks into the water. Bev tried to tempt Emmy.

"Come on, Em, it's beastly hot. It will feel so re-freshing!"

"You go on without me," Emmy said. "I don't want to ruin my curls."

"Oh, Emmy. You're always so proper," Bev splashed her as she dove into the water and Emmy felt a pang of jealousy. She'd never learned to swim. How cool Bev looked in the water. After swim-ming a while, they returned to shore to sunbathe on a large blanket.

"I feel like we're kids again," said Bev. "When was the last time you had such a lazy afternoon?"

Emmy shook her head. She had no idea. Trudy and Catherine joined them, still giggling. "Let me take a photo!" Catherine said. They lay on their stomachs along the beach and propped their chins in their hands.

"Cheese!" said Catherine and snapped a photo. "Trudy, quit blocking your face with your hand."

"But it's so bright! Besides, I think you got your toes in that one," Trudy said.

Emmy agreed. She'd gotten the hang of her little camera, but most people weren't able to properly frame or balance the boxy Brownie while they shot a photo. It had been her stepfather's until he purchased a better one a year ago and sold his old one to Emmy for a dollar. She took it from Catherine and carefully replaced it in her bag. She only had two more exposures for the campout.

Charles strode up to the girls, dripping wet. "Any sandwiches left?" Emmy unwrapped the picnic basket and soon the whole group was eating sandwiches together on the shore

Bill lit up a cigarette and began asking questions. "Why do you think God has allowed the Great Depression to come to the prairies?" Emmy exchanged looks with Bev. What was the point of opening that can of worms?

"My Dad says we got too greedy. Weren't sharing with the rest of the world." Hap said.

"Bad farming practices," said Charles. "That's all there is to it. Bad luck."

"No one knows," said Fred chucking an apple core into the bushes.

"What do you girls think?" Bill smiled.

"I think it's best to leave God's thinking up to

him," Emmy said. "We just have to keep doing our job, loving our neighbour and sharing as best we can."

Bill nodded. "That's a fine sentiment, Emmy." He went on to read some passages in the Bible, urging them to obey God and love their neighbour. It's what they'd heard all their lives. Emmy appreciated that he didn't fill them with guilt at every opportunity. Perhaps it was the fact that he smoked as he talked. Or that he was closer to their age than any minister they'd had before.

They grew hot after half an hour of theological discussion and most of the campers took another dip before returning to camp to rebuild the fire and roast sausages. After praying and tucking in, Bill settled next to Emmy.

"Have you been a camp counsellor before?"

"I've never even been to camp."

Bill lifted his chin toward the other campers. "You have their respect, I can see."

"I've known them all my life," she said. "Probably been their baby-sitter or Sunday School teacher at some point."

Bill flicked the end of his cigarette into the fire. Emmy was beginning to disapprove of how much he smoked. "I'm glad to have you along," he smiled and lay a hand on her shoulder. "You're a great helper."

Emmy couldn't help noticing the nicotine stains on Bill's teeth. She'd hoped to like him better, but he was making it difficult.

"Thank you," she turned away to tidy the mustards and sausage wrappings.

The boys went gopher hunting after dinner leaving the girls on their own.

"How about a nature walk?" Emmy said. They made sure to go in the opposite direction of the hunters.

Catherine and Trudy fell behind a few paces giving Bev and Emmy the chance of a private conversation.

"I'm glad you're here," Bev said. "At least there's one person with sense."

Emmy tucked her hand into her friend's elbow and chuckled. "It's a strange crew, that's for sure. But I'm glad to be independent. Home is no longer home," she sighed.

Bev echoed her sigh. "I wish Howard could have come."

Emmy stopped and studied her friend. "So, you do like him."

Bev tried and failed to supress a grin.

They heard hooting and stopped to follow the sound. Catherine and Trudy caught up to them and Bev pointed at a wide-eyed barn owl at the top of a big Cottonwood tree. Emmy pulled out her binoculars and the girls passed them around. They each had a turn before the owl spread its white wings and took to the air, searching for its dinner.

Emmy pulled a notebook from her pocket and recorded their find. Then, they stopped to pick wild strawberries along the path and stumbled across a green-striped garter snake. Trudy squealed and the snake slithered into the bushes without a sound.

"What if that thing crawls into my sleeping bag tonight?"

"You'd have nothing to fear," said Emmy. "Garter snakes don't bite and they're more afraid of you than you are of them."

Emmy added a Mourning Dove and Mule Deer to their list of sightings before they turned back. They heard several shots as they hiked and returned to a camp full of dead gophers.

"These'll bring in a dollar, at least," Charles said.

"Ever eaten gopher before?" said Fred. "They aren't bad."

Bev blanched. "Oooh, no. Don't eat them. They're full of diseases."

Fred grinned. "No worse than any other prairie animal. They eat our crops. It's just like eating cows or chickens."

Jake spoke up. "Our family lived off gophers one winter. It was all we had."

The group sobered. They'd all suffered in some way from the Depression. Jake's family must have been hit worse than the rest.

The boys skinned the animals, putting aside the tails to be traded when they got to town. Then they grilled them on the fire. The air filled with the scent of roasting meat.

"You ever eaten a gopher before, Emmy?" Bev said, eyes wide.

"Never."

"Well, I'm not doing it," Bev crossed her arms and glared at the fire.

Jake put the grilled gopher on a plate and loaded

the fire with more. "My Ma taught us that wasting is a sin, so everyone, eat up."

The boys all took a gopher, but the girls held back. Jake brought a fresh plate of meat to them. "Come on girls. Tastes a bit like rabbit. I salted them and I swear we never got sick from eating 'em."

He looked so honest and hopeful that Emmy accepted. "You cooked these very well," she smiled. "Thank you, Jake."

Trudy and Catherine each accepted one, but Bev refused. "Suit yourself," said Jake and he returned to the fire.

The boys started an eating contest and Hap won, eating five gophers himself.

"We'll have to leave the rest in the bush," said Bill to Jake. "We don't have enough ice to keep them and we don't want to attract coyotes."

Jake nodded and he and Fred took the rest of the catch far out into the prairies for the animals to eat. Bill pulled out his guitar and Bev seemed to relax as they sang hymns and camp songs. The mosquitoes rose with the setting sun. Emmy and the other girls put on sweaters and pants, but the boys just slapped at the annoying pests and kept singing.

Then Bill began teaching. "Bringing in this large catch of gophers, I couldn't help but think of Jesus' admonition for us to become fishers of men."

He recited several passages of scripture. Emmy wished she could check to see that he had them all right, but it was too dark to read her Bible. It seemed he had a few of the words mixed up. His voice rose with passion the longer he spoke. He'd be an enjoyable preacher one day, but his words left Emmy unmoved. She didn't think he had the correct interpretation of what Jesus meant by becoming fishers of men. One needn't go too far off countries to speak to people in foreign languages. She felt it was much more important to take care of the people around her. Besides, she felt it was a shame the disciples had to leave behind their big catch of fish to become fishers of men. Perhaps they should have taken the fish with them and fed those men first.

After teaching, Bill led them in a long, booming prayer and Emmy's eyes grew heavy. At last he finished, and she forced her eyes open.

"Emmy, perhaps you and the other girls could discuss what you heard from the Lord tonight."

"Of course," she said, grateful to leave the circle. Bev, Trudy and Catherine followed her into their tent.

"Shall we get into our pyjamas first?" she asked and the others agreed. It took a while to get ready by the light of one kerosene lantern, but eventually they snuggled into their camp rolls.

"Pastor Bill certainly has a lot to teach us," Emmy sat cross-legged, afraid she'd fall asleep if she lay down like the others. "Why don't we recite the verse from the Scriptures?"

She read Matthew 19 and they practiced it together a few times.

"I don't think I'd like to go to India or Africa," Trudy said. "It's so far away."

"I don't like to be hot," said Catherine.

Emmy hid a smile. "I think it is quite as worthy to be fishers of men where we are, don't you? Why would God have put us here, in Saskatchewan, if He didn't want us to do his work right here? Bev, how do you think you can do God's work right now?"

She was pleased with the girls' ideas. They all agreed teaching was a worthy profession. She blew out the lantern after a few minutes and they continued sharing thoughts and ideas until they fell asleep.

The next morning, they made bannock over the fire. Emmy and Bev mixed flour, baking soda, salt, lard and water in a large bowl. They kneaded it and took turns wrapping the batter around sticks to roast over the fire. Once it had browned, there was homemade raspberry jam to smother over the fragrant bread. They finished the entire bowl of dough.

"Could you make a little more?" said Hap with a charming, lop-sided smile.

Emmy laughed. "I would have thought your bellies would still be full from your gopher eating contest last night." But she mixed up another batch and they finished that as well.

Bill pulled her aside before beginning their morning teaching session.

"I spoke to one of the girls about your discussion last night," he said, his eyes serious.

"Oh yes?"

"I would prefer it if we were both teaching the same thing."

Emmy turned her eyes away from his penetrating gaze. "I'm not sure what you mean."

"One of our goals is to find missionaries to send out into the field."

Emmy pursed her lips, placed her hands on her hips and returned his gaze. "That is not one of my goals."

Bill cleared his throat. "One of the reasons the denomination sent us out here is to find missionaries."

"Well, they never told me. I'm here to help the girls learn about the Bible and to learn a little myself. I won't be pushing anyone to do something they don't wish to do." She folded her arms in front of her and watched Bill's face grow red. He struggled to reply.

"I'm most disappointed," he said with a huff.

Emmy glared as he shouldered past her.

# CHAPTER TWO

*The Great Commission*

Bill spoke next about the Great Commission from
Christ to go and make disciples of all men. He told
stories of missionaries in Papua New Guinea, Bo-
tswana and India, his face growing red with rising
fervour. He went on longer than he had the night
before, describing the backwardness of the native
peoples and their need for salvation. He told stories
of demon possession and black magic. At first the
others looked frightened and amazed, but as he
continued on, their attention wandered and they
squirmed with discomfort. The sun grew hot. It
was nearly noon. Finally, Emmy stood.

"Thank you, Mr. Withers," she was nearly shouting over his booming voice. "I believe it's nearly
lunch time." Hap smiled at her in relief. "May we
continue with this fascinating topic tonight?"

Bill's eyes grew fierce, but he contained himself

before speaking. "It would be good to take some refreshment. Let us pray."

Emmy felt his prayer was directed at her as he asked God to save the poor lost souls in faraway lands and to make them more aware of the needs of the world, but at last he finished and Emmy hurried away to boil water for tea and potatoes. Bev whispered in her ear.

"Bill seems like a different person, today. What did you say to make him so upset?"

Emmy looked around to make sure no one else could hear. "We disagree on God's essential purpose for the human race."

Bev's eyes were wide, but amusement pulled at her lips. "I didn't know you had it in you, Emmy."

Jake presented three good-sized fish to Emmy just as the water came to a boil. "Thank you. This will make for a more substantial meal."

He had already filleted the perch and she fried them in some oil.

The boys had run off to jump in the water, but they didn't need to be called in for lunch.

Charles held out his plate to be served. "I've worked up quite an appetite."

"If you boys keep eating so much, we're going to have to head home early," she teased. She made sure to give Bill a noticeably smaller piece of fish.

The sound of wheels on gravel drew her eyes to the road. An old Chrysler pulled into their campsite.

"Ah, reinforcements," said Bill as he accepted his lunch.

The car parked beside the other vehicles and young men and women began emerging from within.

A sunburnt man with a large white smile strode toward them. "I see we're just in time." He surveyed the meal being served and patted his stomach.

Emmy steamed. No one had told her to expect more people for lunch.

The sunburnt man chuckled. "Don't worry, Miss. We brought our own food."

Emmy pressed her lips together and smiled. "I'm not worried. We have plenty to share."Her attention was drawn by a tall, gangly figure unfolding himself from the car. He smashed a hat over his head and stretched before making his way toward the camp.

"Why Lars Callas," Emmy said. "I wasn't expecting to see you here."

Lars grinned. "I missed the bush, Miss Bennett. I heard about the church camp and thought it might help."

Bill moved between the two. "How do you know this young man?" Bill's chest seemed fuller than usual.

"We met at church a long time ago," she half-grinned. "He's been up in the bush the last couple of years."

The new campers spread a blanket beside theirs and shared their sandwiches and apples. There was plenty of food and Emmy was pleased to have more girls join their group.

"Emmy, over here," said Bill when she finally

had her plate and was making her way toward the group.

"I'm all right," she said and sat beside Lars instead. Bill's face looked a mixture of anger and hurt. Emmy bit her lip.

"I heard you might be here," Lars said.

"Did you?" She raised her eyebrow at him. "Well you certainly surprised me."

"I thought camping might be a bit like the bush," he said and hid his face in a cup of coffee.

"Do you miss it?" She fiddled with her sandwich.

"Hey Lars, who's your friend?" called the man with the sunburn.

Too many eyes turned their way. Lars's face reddened. "This is Miss Bennett. I met her at the church in Shelby."

"Miss Bennett? So formal, Lars. I think we can use Christian names at camp."

"I'm Emmy," she said, angry at the young man's impertinence. "I'm the women's counsellor."

"Very pleased to make your acquaintance." The man doffed his hat toward her. "I'm the men's counsellor, George. Perhaps you and I could compare notes."

There were a few whistles from the young men. "As long as Bill is present. I'm sure we all want to keep everything appropriate," she said with eyes narrowed.

"Zowie!" one of the new campers clapped George on the back. "She's got your number." Their team had obviously not been given the same speech before they came. The young men seemed determined to flirt.

Bill cut into the exchange. "We're pleased to have you here, George, but I'll need to go over a few rules before you go on."

George's teasing was quashed. "Yes sir. Thank you. I'd like to do my best."

Emmy was momentarily thankful for Bill's commanding nature.

Emmy invited the new girls, Mel and Tina to help with the dishes. She sent the boys to collect water for washing and they heated it over the campfire. Once the washing up was done, they had the afternoon to themselves before supper and the evening study and campfire.

Bev invited the girls to swim the width of the lake and back. Only Mel and Tina joined her.

"I'm no swimmer, Bev," said Trudy. "I'd drown out there in the middle of the lake," she shivered. "I'll just stick to the shore."

"What about you, Emmy?" Mel asked. "It feels like cool silk in here." She bobbed down and up as if to prove what she said.

"No thank you. I'm fine right here," Emmy plunked herself on a blanket, well away from the water.

"She never swims," said Bev, rolling her eyes. "Race you!" The girls took off and Emmy turned her attention to a copy of Shakespeare's As You Like It. She hoped to teach it in the fall and wanted to refresh her memory.

Suddenly, there were hands covering her eyes and bodies dripping cold water all over her. Strong hands reached out to grab her under her arms and around her waist.

"Wait! Stop!" she shouted. She heard Bev's laughter.

"Please. My book!" She let go when someone took As You Like It from her hands, but then she was being lifted toward the water. The hands around her eyes let go as she was lifted up. She saw Bill, Bev, Mel and Hap surrounding her.

"You can't be a teacher at the beach, Emmy. You've got to try the water!"

Emmy pressed her lips together and kicked her legs. "But . . . I . . .can't . . . swim!" She managed just before the tossed her into the lake. She flailed her arms and felt herself sinking into icy depths.

She felt rage and shame at her inability to rescue herself. Her stepfather had taught the other children, but never her.

Then, she felt strong arms around her waist. She gasped when her head emerged into air, but her eyes were squeezed tight against the water.

"I've got you, Miss Bennett. You're okay. Bunch of lunatics." Lars voice, whispering in her ear."Oh Emmy. I'm so sorry. I didn't know you couldn't swim. I just thought you were being prim," Bev whimpered beside her, fussing with her hair and brushing the water away from her eyes. She couldn't be dead. Bev would not be allowed to be her angel after killing her.

"It's okay, you can open your eyes," Lars said.

Emmy opened them and then squeezed them back tight. All around her were the other campers, ogling her humiliation.

"She's all right now," Lars said. "Move out. She doesn't need you all gapping. Go find something to do." Emmy had never heard Lars speak with so much authority.

"I'm alright," she said, suddenly imagining how she looked. "Please put me down."

"With pleasure," Lars said. Emmy made herself open her eyes and noticed how gently Lars set her on her blanket.

"Oh, Emmy. Can you ever forgive me? We just wanted you to enjoy the water. It was all meant in fun," Bev said.

Emmy couldn't reply.

"Why don't you get her a cup of tea," Lars said.

Emmy's face burned as she sat on her blanket. Lars put something around her shoulders and she jumped.

"You're shivering," he said. "Probably the shock. You'll be okay in a bit."

Emmy ran her fingers through her hair. Now all the curl would be gone. She'd have to tie it up in a scarf. She sighed. "I'll suggest separate camps for boys and girls next year."

"Don't do that, Miss Bennett. Who's going to save you if you drown?" Lars said.

Emmy heard the teasing in his reply and whipped her head around, but the look of fear on Lars's face made her relax. He must have surprised even himself with his comment.

"Sorry," he said, fiddling with his hat.

"I'll forgive you this time," she said and smiled.

Lars coughed.

"I'm fine now, thank you. I'd best get back to work."

When they returned, it was time to start supper. The men proudly brought in the fish and gophers they'd caught. No one brought more than Lars.

"Murder!" yelled Hap. "You really know how to bring in the goods."

Lars scratched his head and scrunched his forehead. "I wouldn't call it murder, pal. Just a bit of hunting and fishing."

Fred and Charles laughed and slapped their friend on the back. "He just means he's impressed. Heard the expression at a picture, I think."

Lars grinned. "I must have missed that picture."

Lars also had a handkerchief full of berries. He made himself a spot in the midst of the girls to skin the two hares he caught and gut the fish. Emmy reached out to take a fillet to cook for supper, but Lars caught her wrist.

"You don't think I can cook?" His eyes twinkled.

Emmy's eyes widened. "Really?"

He let her go and wiped his hands on a rag. "I cooked for a team of men up in the bush my first year. I learned to make a mean pie. Could I use some of the lard and flour?"

Emmy put her hands on her hips and tried to make sense of what she was hearing. She opened one hand and gestured to the food rations. "Help yourself. I'll believe it when I see it."

She and the other girls continued preparing dinner. They fried fish, game and potatoes, but Emmy kept an eye on Lars. His filets and meat were cut neatly in uniform shape. He set them to the side with some salt and turned his attention to the pie. He cleaned and dried a smooth board and began mixing flour, salt and sugar together. He cut in the lard with two knives. He mixed in a bit of cool lake water, kneaded it briefly and set it to the side. Then, he washed and dried the berries, mixed them in a bowl with some flour and sugar, and covered them with a cloth to keep out the flies.

Next, Lars chopped potatoes and carrots and placed them in a cast iron pan with his rabbit. He tended to them carefully and added the fish fillets once the rabbit started to brown. He kept an eye on the fire and rolled out his pie dough. Emmy noted the dough was smooth and even as Lars formed a pie shell in some tin foil. He took his meat and potatoes out of the fire and set them in a dish. Then he placed the tinfoil in the pan and added the berries, topping it with the other rolled piece of dough. He placed another pan on top and set the whole thing in the glowing coals.

"Pie should be ready in time for dessert," he said.

Emmy tried not to gape. His meal looked more appetizing than anything she'd made.

Bill muttered "I wouldn't trust a meal made by a man." But after he said grace over the meal, Emmy noticed he selected all of Lars's dishes.

"How did I do?" Lars grinned at Emmy. They sat together on the picnic blanket.

Emmy smiled. "You put those other boys to shame." She nodded her chin in Bill's direction but spoke softly enough so only Lars would hear. "And us girls too."

"I don't know why more men don't take up cooking. It's relaxing."

Lars leaned on one elbow and began to eat, but whenever someone spoke to him, he left his fork on his plate, listening and responding. Everyone else finished long before he did.

"Would you like some more?" Emmy offered to take his plate. Lars surveyed the leftovers.

"Don't mind if I do."

Emmy refilled his plate while Lars took a look at his pie.

"Not ready yet," he said. They sat together while the sun set; golden light dancing over the calm lake, pink, yellow and orange blooming behind the low hills.

"I'm glad you came to camp," Emmy said. "To help with the cooking," she hurried to add.

Lars wouldn't meet her eyes and took his time replying. "I can do other things too." Then he looked at her with a dopey grin.

Emmy felt her cheeks flush but Bill interrupted to insist they clean up before it got dark. Emmy wanted to tell Bill to clean up himself, but she held her tongue and organized the girls. Within minutes, Lars joined them in washing and drying the dishes. The other girls giggled and tried flirting with Lars, but he only nodded and completed his task. Then he checked his pie and announced it was finished. Bill was first in line, but Lars stopped him from digging in.

"Sorry, chum. I made this one for the cooks to-night. I have to pass their standards before I make one for everyone else."

Bill set down his plate and moved aside for the ladies.

They each took a small piece and left a large slice for Lars. "Won't you have some?" Emmy asked when he made no motion to take it.

"Not me. I know how my pies taste. What do you say?"

"Excellent." She grinned. "Almost as good as my mother's."

"I'll have to learn her secret." Lars nodded and moved away from Emmy. Emmy took the last piece of pie to Bill who needed only a little encouragement to accept.

By the next afternoon, Emmy was growing weary of so many people. Although Bill had put a damper on a lot of the teasing and flirting, it was still happening in a more subdued manner. Instead of joining everyone on the beach, she took a walk through the coulees. It was hot for walking, but a breeze kept her from being uncomfortable. She enjoyed the silver leaves of the wolf willow and the puckering taste of a few chokecherries as she walked. It was good to be alone with only the gentle wind and the odd hawk to break through her thoughts.

She was following the sound of some rustling in

the bushes when Lars emerged with a bashful grin. She jumped.

"Sorry to break into your thoughts, Miss." He touched the brim of his hat.

"Have you been here long?"

"I noticed you coming this way about half an hour ago."

"Why didn't you wave?" She crossed her arms, feeling exposed.

"Trying to outwait a red fox I spotted an hour ago. It would bring in a nice price. Not a scratch on him."

"An hour is a long time to wait." Emmy relaxed.

"Not so long," Lars said. "I've waited a full day up North. And in much colder weather."

"When will you go back?"

"Up north, you mean?" He scratched the back of his neck.

Emmy nodded.

"I'd say that part of my life is done." He gazed into the distance.

"Really? But I thought you loved it."

Lars flopped onto the grass, selected a piece, and chewed on it. Emmy tucked her dress beneath her knees and knelt beside him.

"The north was a wonderful adventure, but it's time I grew up." He nodded as if agreeing with someone unseen.

"Trapping is hardly child's play."

"Canada may enter the war soon enough. I expect my skills will come in handy." He gazed at her as if measuring her response.

Despite the wavering heat, Emmy's hands grew cold. She'd heard rumours as well, but Lars made it sound like a certainty. Most of her young brothers would be eligible to fight and she wouldn't blame them for wanting to strike out on their own.

"Seems a shame."

Lars reached for her hand and held it. She looked at him in surprise but did not pull away. "Would you miss me if I went?" he said after several minutes.

Emmy cleared her throat, which had grown thick. "Yes. I expect I would."

Lars grinned. "That's good to hear, Emmy."

Emmy opened her mouth to put him in place. It was the first time he had called her by her Christian name. But his face looked so earnest, she closed her mouth again, a feeling of warmth spreading over her limbs.

# CHAPTER THREE

*Sun•ay*

Camp and all thoughts of Lars faded into memories when Emmy returned home to prepare for work.

Harding had a big enough school to boast four classrooms. In the last two weeks of August, Emmy and Bev met when they could to share ideas and plans. They would both be teaching the younger students.

"What have they offered to pay you?" Emmy asked the evening before they were to leave.

"$20 a month. They said we would all make the same salary," Bev said.

"Yes, they told me the same thing. I just wanted to make sure."

Bev patted her hand. "It's an honest school board."

Emmy stood to stretch. "I hope so, Bev. I need an income."

Bev gazed out the window. Howard was coming

in from the fields. "Do you really think Canada will join the war?"

Emmy pursed her lips. She couldn't bear to imagine her little brothers fighting across the ocean. Or Lars. "Our European brothers and sisters need help. We can't allow Hitler to take control."

Bev sighed.

"I'll go make tea," Emmy said. "Maybe if we keep praying, this war will end soon."


Lars arrived at her home early on Sunday morning. "Someone to see you, Emmy," her mother called from the door. Emmy bit her lip. He was too early. She hadn't had time to do her hair or to tell her parents about him.

"Be out in a moment," she called from her bedroom. She hurried to finish. She hated to leave him alone with her step-father, Owen.

When she came to the kitchen, Lars gripped a cup of coffee between white hands.

"So, you've given up, then," Owen said.

"Most white trappers don't stay as long as we did," Lars replied after a pause.

"I never gave up on anything in my life," Owen's chest was puffed out. "Been farming since I was a kid. All through this blasted Depression, never gave up."

"That's admirable, sir," said Lars.

"Good morning," Emmy broke in. "Can I get you some eggs?"

"Already on the way," her mother smiled. "Why

don't you sit with Mr. Callas, Emmy. Mary and Jean can help this morning."

Emmy accepted her own cup of coffee. "Lars was at camp with me this summer," she began.

"So he said," Owen grunted.

"He caught most of our fish and game," she said, purposely leaving out his cooking and baking skills.

"Don't you have a brother?" Owen peered at him.

"Yes, my brother Earl," said Lars. "I'm afraid he's not well. I came on my own this morning, to take Emmy to church."

Emmy's mother and step-father exchanged looks. She and Lars had called one another by their Christian names in front of her parents.

Owen sat up in his chair and leaned closer to Lars. "Listen, son. I won't have a drifter courting my daughter." His face was red.

"I'm no drifter, sir," Lars said with a steady gaze. "I've been working at the family farm since I returned. My family's been settled in Red Lily for twenty years."

Mary and Jean placed plates of eggs, toast and fried tomatoes in front of Emmy, her father and Lars, but no one joined them at the breakfast table.

Owen tore his eyes from Lars to stare at Emmy. "Why didn't you tell us you had a fella," he said.

"I meant to this morning," she said. "Lars arrived earlier than I thought."

"I'm sorry." Lars stood and bumped his head on the low-hung lamp.

Emmy watched him rub his head with a mixture

of pity and anger. "It's not your fault. Please stay. I should have told them."

Lars looked as if he couldn't decide whether to sit or run away.

"Please?"

Lars accepted her request and sat. It was silent as the rest of the family drifted to the table. Her step-father said grace and they ate quietly for several uncomfortable minutes.

"This is a fine breakfast," Lars said.

"Thank you, Lars." Her mother smiled.

"Emmy tells me you bake a mean pie."

Her mother smiled at Emmy. "Did she now? Well, I'll have to make one for you. Can you come for dinner?"

Her step-father grunted.

"That would be grand," Lars said. Emmy relaxed an inch. He was no coward. She had to give him that.


Lars had brought a horse and cart to take Emmy to church. A meadowlark trilled in the early morning stillness.

"Do you plan to stay on your family's farm?" she said.

"For now, but I'm getting antsy. I haven't been home this long since I was in school."

The road was dusty, but not as bad as it had been previous summers.

"When do you head out to teach?"

Emmy fiddled with her purse. "I go to Harding tomorrow."

Lars stopped on the road, looking as though he wanted to say something. Just then, Emmy's brothers raced past them.

"What's the problem, Lars?" Howard hollered as they ran. "Cat got your tongue?"

"Why don't you just kiss her?" said Jack, but he was already too far away for Emmy to scold him.

Lars's cheeks were red, but he controlled his voice. "You'll make a fine teacher." He made sure Emmy's brothers were out of sight before he reached to take her hand.

# CHAPTER FOUR

---

*Abyssinia*

"Abyssinia," said Becky. Her bare foot dangled as she perched on her older sister's iron bed.

"Don't use slang," said Emmy as she checked the contents of her suitcase one last time.

"But everyone says it. Do you know what it means?"

"I'll be seeing you," Emmy enunciated.

"See! You know it. Come on. Say it just once. It can be our secret."

Emmy stopped her checking and looked at her twinkly-eyed youngest sibling. Emmy pursed her lips together. "It's not proper."

Becky's smile drooped.

"Wagon's here," Emmy's stepfather, Owen said from his rocking chair in the parlour, where he could see everyone coming and going.

Emmy kissed her sister goodbye, gripped her

suitcase and hurried out of the room they'd shared all of Becky's life.

"'Bout time you earned your own way," Owen said without emotion.

"Yes sir," she said. This was the safest response, although if she used it too often he would start mocking her, like a parrot.

"My dear," her mother approached in the privacy of the coatroom, out of sight. "Here's a little something." She whispered and passed over a handkerchief, embroidered with her late father's initials. "Don't open it until you're alone." Her eyes were misty as she embraced Emmy. Her mother scurried away before Owen scolded her for mollycoddling her eldest.

"Hurry up, girl," Owen said.

Emmy ducked outside without saying goodbye. She didn't want her stepfather to shame her for the tears in her eyes. She patted her headscarf to make sure it held her dark curls in place, straightened her shoulders and marched toward her future.

"Emmy Bennett?" the driver asked.

"Yes," she said.

"I'm Mr. Blaine. That all you got?" He eyed her small case. "I hope it'll be enough. Gets real cold where you're heading and people aren't keen to share the little they have."

"I'm not expecting any handouts." Emmy climbed into the rough wagon. Mr. Blaine didn't get out of his seat or offer her a hand up.

Mr. Blaine clucked his tongue at the horses and they left Emmy's home behind.

Emmy gazed at the ripe fields and wide prairie as the wagon jostled and bumped down the long, dusty road. Mr. Blaine was largely taciturn, for which she was grateful. They picked up Bev down the road and Emmy allowed herself the smallest degree of relaxation. They couldn't speak freely in front of Mr. Blaine and, after a mostly sleepless night, Emmy nodded off in the bumpy wagon.

She jolted awake, noting the movement of the sun when she did.

"I hope you aren't expecting a life of leisure," Mr. Blaine said when she woke.

Emmy sat up straighter. Bev patted her hand.

At noon, Emmy opened the lunch hamper her mother had filled with scones, meat pies, bread, cookies and cheese. There was enough for her whole family. It was a sacrifice so she would have a taste of home. She ate, sharing with Bev and Mr. Blaine as her mother instructed. Bev had brought food as well, but Emmy insisted Bev keep the food for her host family. After they ate their fill, Emmy's basket remained full.

"Your mother's a fine cook," Mr. Blaine said. "Hope she's passed on the skill."

"Thank you." It wasn't Emmy's job to cook and clean for her host family. Mr. Blaine was sadly mistaken if he expected her to do so.

She was beginning to crave tea when the town of Harding came into view. It looked a lot like Shelby. The church steeple rose above all other buildings except the grain elevator and the same train tracks connected the two towns. She knew there'd be a general store, a bank and a post office, but she wasn't sure of the most important feature.

"Is there a curling rink?" she asked as they turned off the main road.

Mr. Blaine cleared his throat. "No time for such fripperies in Harding. You'll have to make do with school dances for your entertainment. You two and the other teachers will be in charge of organizing those."

Emmy felt deflated but she ignored the sensation. "Of course," she shook her head. "I'm sure it's a fine town."

"A town's only as fine as its people, Miss Bennett."

Emmy felt this was a warning.

Mrs. Blaine was cooking over an ancient stove when they entered the farmhouse. The rank smell of old cabbage and burnt potatoes filled Emmy's nostrils. There was no wallpaper and a stack of dishes nearly tottered in the sink. They had dropped Bev off with her hosts the Fells beforehand, leaving Emmy with no support as she took in the squalor.

A toddler with a runny nose clung to his mother's dress. He hid his face when Emmy appeared, smearing his mother's already filthy skirt. A small girl with unkempt hair held a baby in her lap on a wooden chair by the unset table, reminding Emmy of herself holding her sister Becky. Emmy looked for other children who might be old enough to help their mother get supper, but she couldn't find any. Emmy put on a tight smile and offered her hand to her hostess.

"Good evening Mrs. Blaine," she said. "Nice to meet you."

Mrs. Blaine cast a suspicious eye over Emmy's proffered hand and then her attire. "I trust you had a good ride."

"Yes, thank you."

"A whole day's work lost," she muttered into the concoction on the stove.

"That's not for you to worry about, Millie," Mr. Blaine shook his head at his wife.

Millie put down her spoon and wiped her hands on a crusted apron. "I'll show you to your room."

Emmy kept her coat as they squeezed through the kitchen into a small parlour and then down the hall to two bedrooms.

"This one'll be yours," she motioned to a tiny room. "We've the privy in the back. Bath's every two weeks in the kitchen. Girls first and then the boys." Emmy tried not to shudder.

"Me and Frank are across the hall and the children sleep in the loft above," she pointed to a ladder. Emmy climbed it with her eyes.

"How many children do you have?" she asked.

"Nine," she said and left.

Emmy's room contained a single brass bed with a handmade quilt and rough sheets. The quilt was a thin, faded and peach-coloured. There was a chest of drawers that took some effort to open. In the corner behind the door was a basin on a handmade stand and a wavy mirror nailed to the wall. She'd have a hard time doing her hair, but at least she had a room to herself.

Emmy placed her case on the bed and removed its contents into the musty drawers. A small curtainless window revealed vast, withered fields. The fields had looked this way before the destructive dust storms a few years back. Once, she'd walked home from school with Becky when the clouds blew in. They'd held tightly to their horse Briony as the dry dirt filled their eyes, nose and ears. They couldn't see a thing and Briony whined and wriggled while they patted her to keep her calm. Who would make sure Becky survived if such a catastrophe returned?

"Abyssinia," she said.

Emmy had likely displaced some of the Blaine children from this room. She wished she had brought along an extra blanket and some cloth for the window. She wouldn't be going home until Christmas. She couldn't say Mr. Blaine hadn't warned her. She removed her coat and slouch hat and hung them on a rusty nail protruding from the wall. There was water in the ewer and she did her best to clean the dust from her hands and face before searching for the outhouse.

The rest of the children showed up for supper, not tea. Nine children and three adults squeezed around the wobbly table. Mrs. Blaine told them to wash up before they sat, but Emmy could see most of them still had dirt under their fingernails and smudges on their faces. They carried the scents of dust and mud.

"Say hello to your new teacher, children," Mrs. Blaine said while she ladled steaming soup into chipped bowls.

"I'm Cassie," a skinny girl smiled up at Emmy with a toothless grin.

"I'm Miss Bennett," Emmy smiled back.

"Yeah, we know," said the oldest boy. He wore a dirty collared shirt under a pair of dungarees. "I'm Sam."

"Hello Sam," Emmy refrained from shaking their dirty hands. She wanted to avoid illness before the school year started. Instead, she nodded at them as they said their names.

They watched their father fold his hands together and followed his example. Emmy closed her eyes and listened.

"For what we are about to receive, may the Lord make us truly grateful," said Mr. Blaine. "Amen."

Emmy had the feeling he was praying for her benefit. When she reopened her eyes, the children were madly tucking into their supper.

Emmy took up her own spoon, ignored the spots, and tasted the soup. Her thin and flavourless bowl held more meat than any of the children's. She was touched by the generosity, but if this was their best, what would happen when they returned to their everyday habits?

After they'd eaten every scrap of soup, Emmy

cut them each a slice of the fruit-cake her mother had sent. The children sighed over each mouthful. When they had finished, Emmy offered to help with the dishes.

"You're our guest today," Mrs. Blaine said. "We'll sort how you can help later. You've had a long journey and you'll be needing some rest. I have the girls." She nodded at her pale daughters. The oldest was likely eight. No wonder the dishes were piled up.

"You'll be wanting to get to work, then," Mr. Blaine said. "We expect our teachers to spend most of their spare time planning and marking. You'll have a half day off on Sundays, but we expect you to work as hard as the rest of us.

Emmy bristled at the suggestion she was lazy, but she bit her tongue and thanked Mrs. Blaine for supper before leaving the kitchen.

Back in her room, Emmy reviewed her lesson plans. She'd worked on them throughout the summer but wondered if they would suit her new students. There was no way of knowing how many would be in each grade. Hopefully, she'd find a register at school the next morning.

She went over the list of rules for a female teacher which expressly forbade her from marrying during her year of teaching. It also required she be at home between 8 p.m. and 6 a.m. preparing her lessons, unless attending a school function.

"No problem there," she said into the empty room. After folding the documents away, she cleaned her face and teeth, pulled on her nightgown and settled into her creaky bed.

Finally, she pulled her mother's gift from her pocket. She unfolded the embroidered handkerchief and found a gold necklace with a bell-shaped pendant. Inscribed on the back were the words "For Miss Bell, the best teacher." Her mother had never told her she'd been a school teacher. Emmy refused to let herself cry with the rush of homesickness this brought. Mr. Blaine wasn't any worse than her father. But Mrs. Blaine was no replacement for her mother.

# CHAPTER FIVE

*Harⅰing School*

"Miss Bennett?" a round man with red cheeks and a ready smile held out his hand when Emmy met him at the door. Behind him, she could see Bev waving from a fine wagon.

"I'm Mr. Fell," he said, shaking her hand. She followed him to the wagon as he continued talking.

"I thought I'd give you and Miss Lafferty a little tour of Harding before I show you the school. Have you been here before?"

Emmy shook her head. She was grateful for Bev's familiar face after a night with strangers. Mr. Fell kept up a lively conversation, pointing out landmarks on their way into town. Once there, he pointed out the town's restaurant, post office, general store, bank and hardware store as they drove.

"It's bigger than Shelby," Bev remarked.

"Is that right?" Mr. Fell nodded. "Well, that's about it. I'll take you to the school next. I expect you're anxious to get started."

Emmy smiled at Bev, a flutter of excitement overtaking some of her nerves.

"Here's your school then," Mr. Fell pulled on the reins to stop the horses.

Mr. Fell helped them out of the carriage as he talked about the school. "The Old, Old School was built in 1900. Only two years later, we needed a new school. The second was called the Stone School, but wouldn't you know, only a decade later, our town was busting with kids and they built this, The Brick School in 1913. Four rooms, you know." His puffed his chest and rocked up onto his toes, before unlocking the building.

"This here will be your classroom, Miss Lafferty," he said, consulting a folded piece of paper. "Grades 4 to 6. You'll have my Dory in your class."

"Very nice," Bev said as she took in the musty classroom with its rows of desks, teacher stage and chalkboard. "How forlorn a classroom looks without any children."

"I suppose it does," Mr. Fell stroked his moustache.

"Miss Bennett, you're across the hall with the little 'uns," he said and unlocked Emmy's classroom. It looked much the same, but with smaller desks. Her hands itched to dust and sweep, but she knew they had more to see and do before they could set to work.

They toured the rest of the building which included a teacher's lounge and indoor bathroom.

"I know you'd like to settle in," Mr. Fell said.

"Mrs. Fell and the children are expecting you for lunch. You can come by at noon."

He disappeared, and Bev took the chance to hug Emmy. "Our own classrooms, Em!"

"An indoor bathroom. Heavenly."

Bev and Emmy spent the morning dusting, rearranging and preparing the school for the students who would begin the next day. During a break from cleaning, Emmy surveyed her desk. The heavy, scuffed monstrosity was placed before the chalkboard at the front of the classroom. A quick look through the desk revealed last year's roll, a dried-up inkwell, and a single sheet of paper.

1938-39 Miss Miller.
Covered War of 1812, Kings of England, British and Canadian Geography.

"An entire year summed up in one sentence," she muttered to herself. Later that week, she would test the children to see what they remembered on these subjects from their former teacher.

Just before eleven, two women strode into the school, their eyes narrowed. Bev and Emmy hurried from their classrooms to greet them.

"I'm Bev and this is my friend Emmy. We're excited to be teaching with you this year." Bev was friendly despite their cool looks.

"I'm Anne and this is Mel." Anne extended her hand. She was small and round with glasses and fierce-looking eyebrows. Mel inched toward them, tall and thin. Then the women walked on to the upper classrooms down the hall and peered inside.

"Look, girls," Anne said. "It's tradition here for the first-year teachers to clean the upper classrooms as well." She grinned at Mel, who raised her eyebrows in surprise.

"Really, Anne?"

"Yes, that's right. We have so much to prepare in teaching the older students. I hope you understand."

Emmy saw through Anne's little ruse. "Well, I'm sure you'll agree that's a ridiculous tradition, but why don't we have some tea and get to know one another." She bustled past Anne and Mel toward the Teacher's Lounge, ignoring the look of disapproval on Anne's face. She smiled, pleased she'd set the tone and boundaries for the year.

"I'll call when it's ready. Give you some time to settle in." She called behind her and got to work on a little fire.

A quarter of an hour later, they sat around the small table, their knees bumping into one another. Emmy wondered what they would do if they ever had guests.

"Would anyone like some lemon in their tea?" She held up her yellow squeeze bottle. Bev agreed but the other two shook their heads.

"Did you both teach here last term?" Bev asked Anne and Mel.

Anne stirred cream and sugar into her tea before she answered. "Yes. I taught your class, Beverly, and Mel taught Emmy's class."

"What made you want to go up?" Bev passed around a plate of cookies her mother had sent.

"Higher pay, naturally," said Mel.

"We were told that everyone is paid the same," Emmy said.

Mel and Anne shrugged. "That's what they say, but it's not true."

Bev held a cookie halfway up to her mouth. "But we will be paid what they promised?"

Anne had an entire cookie in her mouth, but merely pushed it into her cheek and spoke anyway. "Yes, you will be paid," she said as crumbs sprayed from her lips. "But we couldn't put up with such a pittance again."

"So, is it much more money in the higher grades?"

Mel's laugh grated. "You betcha! Almost double."

Emmy stood and put her hands on her hips. "Well of all the dirty tricks. . ."

Bev held out her hand and rested it on Emmy's elbow. "Now, don't get all worked up.

Maybe there's a mistake."

Emmy began pacing the tiny room, straightening dishes as she went.

"You see, she's hoping to be independent from her step-father." Emmy gave her friend a hard look. She didn't need these strange women knowing her business.

Emmy stopped pacing. "I'll take it up at the next school board meeting." She refilled everyone's teacup.

Anne's lip curled with mischief. "Why don't you just do that." She drained her teacup. "Thank you for the tea. I'd best get on with things." She left the table without washing out her teacup and Mel soon followed.

Bev watched them and ate another cookie. "Might be a long semester with those two."

Emmy cleared the dishes. "We'll just think of them as some of our students. We must bring them to hand." Yet she was too shaken to insist they clean their tea things. She'd do it herself today and make sure they took on their share of work later.

The Fells had five children, four of school age. Mr. Fell owned the town's General Store which must be doing well as they ate a large and delicious dinner of roast beef, potatoes, gravy, three salads, a tomato aspic and coffee with cream and sugar. Emmy couldn't remember the last time she'd had such a heavy meal at midday.

The children were, for the most part, polite and well-behaved, but Emmy felt some small sense of dread. Soon she would have a classroom full of children who would be testing her boundaries at school, but she brushed it away and threw herself into a game of Parcheesi with the three eldest Fell children after dinner.

At 1:00, Mr. Fell announced he needed to return to his store for the afternoon. "You won't see much of me, unless you come to the store. It's my most demanding child. Can't leave it alone for long." He chuckled, combed his moustache once more and bid them a good afternoon.

Robins woke Emmy before the rooster could. She sat with sore muscles and a cricked neck after her day of cleaning and preparation. The sun struggled to shine through the early morning dust haze. Her lesson plans lay scattered on her thin comforter and she gathered them into a neat pile. Then she stretched her foot onto the bare floor, almost inspired to return to bed for the day by the frigid planks of wood. Instead, she hastened to find her stockings and pulled them on beneath her nightgown. She removed her coat from the nail on the wall and did her best to drape it over the window for privacy. After she finished dressing and washing, she stepped out to use the outhouse.

On opening the rough grey door, she found Cassie, one of the youngest girls, sitting inside. Emmy let the door bang shut.

"Good morning, Miss," the child said.

Emmy struggled to keep her voice calm. "You'll need to lock the door now that I'm here," she said.

Cassie laughed. "Okay, Miss. But what if I get locked in? I don't want to climb down into the hole." A second later she was outside, grinning.

"Here, I'll show you," Emmy said. She took the girl back inside and showed her how to use the latch and had her practice several times.

"Okay, I'll use it then. If I remember." Cassie skipped back to the house.

In the kitchen, Mrs. Blaine looked exhausted and frazzled. She had eight lunch pails before her and something bubbling on the stove. Emmy bit her lip. She wanted to take over but was afraid to start the precedent. She'd come here to teach, not to be a Mother's helper.

"Good morning," Emmy said. "Shall I set the table?"

"Suit yourself," Mrs. Blaine said. Her face was blank, like something was missing.

Emmy set out the dishes. Then she stirred the oatmeal and fetched the milk from the icebox while Mrs. Blaine struggled over the lunch pails. There didn't seem to be much to put inside. Emmy remembered the leftovers from her mother's packed lunch and provided them to Mrs. Blaine who divided them amongst the pails.

"I'll call the children," Emmy said.

Emmy strode toward the ladder and called into the loft. "Time to wash up and come to breakfast," she said.

Cassie was the only one who washed her hands and so Emmy reminded each of the other children. They looked at their mother to see if they needed to obey their new house guest, but Mrs. Blaine stared out the window. "Come along, then." Emmy said.

Eventually all nine children were washed and seated. Emmy was ladling out the oatmeal when Mr. Blaine came in. She noticed he didn't wash his hands, but she dared not admonish him.

He saw her serving. "Eh, Millie, that's not Miss Bennett's job."

Mrs. Blaine snapped to attention and reached to take the pot from Emmy's hands.

"It's alright. I don't expect to be served," Emmy said. "It's a lot for one woman to do alone."

Mr. Blaine frowned at Emmy. "You suggesting I make her work too hard?"

"No, I..."

"I don't know what your Father was like, but around here, you'll need to respect the head of the house."

He skipped grace and the family dug into their breakfast. The children looked at one another with wide eyes but said nothing. The porridge made a painful rock in Emmy's stomach, but she finished every bite.

Mr. Blaine ate quickly and then pushed his chair back and stood, towering over them. "I don't plan to drive you when the weather's fine. The children usually walk."

"I enjoy the exercise." Emmy refused to give Mr. Blaine the satisfaction of belittling her.

He pressed his lips together. "The boys can go to school today, but I'll be needing them when the harvest is ready." He strode outside.

Emmy stood with her hands on her hips. Even her step-father knew the importance of good school attendance. "Every child deserves an education, sir."

Mr. Blaine stopped in the doorway. "Pardon me?"

"Children have the right to go to school. They fall behind when they miss even one day."

Mr. Blaine sneered and stepped toward her with a finger crooked in her direction. "Listen, Miss Bennett, I don't know what kind of home you come from, but in our home, the man is the head of the household. You'll need to learn to respect that or you can find yourself another place to stay." He took another step toward Emmy. "I am also the head of the school board, which means if you can't respect my authority as the head of this house, you will respect my authority over your job. There are plenty of women out there who can fill your job. Do we have an understanding, Miss Bennett?"

Emmy steamed with anger inside, but she nodded. He stared at her until she looked away and then huffed out the door. Her legs wobbled beneath her, but she shook her head and turned her thoughts toward her first day.

Fifteen minutes later, Emmy stood by the front door with a fluttering heart and a scrubbed face. She looked to see how many children were ready. Seven were of school age, but only three were there.

"I'll be leaving in two minutes," Emmy said. Mrs. Blaine was nursing the baby in the corner of the kitchen with her eyes closed. Emmy would not call for the children. If Mrs. Blaine wanted them to go with her, she'd have to gather them herself.

Emmy grabbed her coat, hat, satchel and lunch pail and tied her shoes. She set off in the direction of the school. The older boys tore out in front of her and the other five fell in behind. She marched several yards along the dusty path when she felt a soft hand in hers, melting some of the anger she was nursing toward Mr. Blaine.

"Good morning, Miss," Cassie gave her a toothless grin.

"It's going to be a great day."

"Yes, I know," she bobbed her head. "I get to bring the new teacher to school."

Emmy chuckled and watched a Red-Tailed Hawk circling overhead.

Three miles passed before Emmy saw the tall brick schoolhouse. It was raised above the rest of the flat land, built to withstand wind and weather. A wide white staircase led up to the austere building. Five students were waiting on the stairs. Bev had joined Emmy along the way. They had thought they'd be the first to arrive first with time to prepare, but a new teacher was a curiosity. Three girls ran to meet them on the road while the two boys stayed back to scuff their shoes in the dust.

"Good morning Misses. Mother sent these for you." The tallest girl held out two apples. Long dark plaits hung down either side of her dress.

"Thank you. I'm Miss Bennett and this is Miss Lafferty. What is your name?" She held out her hand in greeting.

The girl grinned and shook her teacher's hand. "I'm Patsy. This here is Jane and Betsy and the two boys are Frank and Bert, our brothers."

Emmy and Bev smiled at each child. "Well, I

expect we could use your help, if you're willing. You as well." Emmy nodded at the Blaine children. "Let's see how the school looks."

She pulled out the key Mr. Fell had given her the day before. The door clicked open and something scurried away as they entered the school. The children crowded into the tiny mudroom with her, stomping their boots and shoes before they entered.

"Who can show me where to store the lunch pails?" Bev said, swallowing her nerves.

All the girls called out and she chose Jane to point out a rough shelf at the back of the room.

"Miss Miller figured this was the best place to keep our food away from flies," she said. Emmy and the girls put their pails in a row. The boys lagged behind.

"Sam, will you take one of the older boys to the barn and see if the stalls are in good order?" Emmy said. Sam's chest seemed to puff out in pride and he took Bert along.

"Tommy, could you find the broom and have someone help you sweep up the classrooms. There might be mouse droppings."

The boys grumbled but followed her directions. A few other children poked their heads into the door and she motioned for them to enter. Dahlia and Rosemond joined the other girls wiping desks. Emmy sent Georgia and Alastair to fetch water for cleaning as well as to fill up the drinking pail.

"Looks like you'll need to wash up the ladle and tin cup as well," Emmy said when she saw the dust and dead flies within.

Once all the children were working, Emmy pulled her lesson plans from her satchel and found a blank piece of paper to begin her new roll for the year. She had fourteen students already.

The shelf of readers revealed only a few torn and yellowed copies for each grade level. She pulled Book One off the shelf and brought it to her desk. She copied the Lord's Prayer and Maple Leaf Forever onto the blackboard. There were a few short pieces of chalk left and no new scribblers. She made a note to have them ordered as soon as possible.

The classroom was getting noisy and she turned to find more children had arrived. "Please come forward and state your name," she said. Two new boys studied her a moment before following her directions.

"Oscar Fleishman," said the oldest with a heavy German accent. "This is my brother Robert."

Emmy added their names to the roll and asked them to check that each desk had a slate. Oscar nodded with a stern expression and then whispered the instructions in German to his younger brother.

She sent the children outside to play and took a few minutes to review her lesson plans, making additional notes and changes as she read. Of course, everything would change, but it was important to know her plans well so that she could easily adapt them. She added additional lines to her class register in case of new students and then began copying out the day's work on the blackboard.

When Emmy finished, she stepped across the hallway to see Bev.

"Are you okay?" she asked when she saw her friend's hand trembling along the blackboard.

Bev plunked the chalk onto the ledge and curled and flexed her right hand. "First day jitters are all," she said with a quavering laugh. "I just need the day to begin and distract me from my nerves."

"Let me help," Emmy took up the abandoned chalk and Bev handed over the math problems she'd been scribing.

"You're so organized and calm. How do you do it?"

"I don't feel calm," Emmy said. "I'll make us some tea," she said once she'd finished the copying.

She passed by Anne and Mel's classrooms on her way to the small Teacher's lounge. She couldn't help noticing both rooms looked as dismal and disused as they had the day before. Neither Mel nor Anne were in their rooms. Instead, they sat in the Teacher's lounge, smoking.

Emmy coughed and waved away the smelly cloud. "Good morning. Are you sure you're allowed to smoke at school?"

Anne waved her hand through the air. "No one's ever complained. They've no right to tell us what we can and can't do in our spare time."

"Besides," Mel said, her finger pressed into her temple. "It's completely healthful."

Emmy found two chipped mugs and escaped the cramped room as quickly as possible. She did not plan to return. She made tea in the classroom with the water she boiled on her wood stove. It wasn't necessarily cold enough to light the stove, but she'd found plenty of wood and matches and was in desperate need of hot tea after her sleepless night. She carried the mugs into Bev's classroom and found her watching the children out the window.

"Here they come," she said, accepting one of the mugs. "Thank you. What a treat."

"Mel and Anne have done nothing in their classrooms," Emmy said. "I wonder how they plan to make it through the day."

Bev took a long sip of her tea. "Let's meet the children. Will you come out with me?"

Emmy blew on her own tea. "In a minute. I want to be at my best. Tea first."

Boys and girls came from all directions and met in clusters to talk or play hopscotch, jacks or tag. A few girls peered into the windows and Bev waved.

"Best not to encourage that," Emmy said. "They'll do it all year long."

Bev set her half-finished mug on her desk. "I can't wait any longer. I have to go outside."

Emmy chuckled at her friend's enthusiasm and carried her own mug to her classroom. She surveyed the classroom, satisfied it was beginning to take shape. Then she found her hat, pinned it in place and joined Bev on the steps to greet their students.

Emmy pulled out her pocket watch and saw they had ten minutes until school began. It was going to be a warm day. There would be no need to keep her woodstove burning.

Just then, a matronly woman with greying hair tied in a thin bun marched into the classroom.

"Good morning, Miss Bennett," her voice had a Scottish lilt which immediately reminded Emmy of her mother. "Looks like you're getting this place into order. I'm Mary Drummond."

"Emmy Bennett," she replied and shook the woman's hand.

"My husband is on the school board," she said, then lowered her voice and hid her mouth behind her hand. "Though I'm the one who attends the meetings for him." She winked and returned to a normal volume. "I've come to see that you have everything you need."

Emmy reached for her list. "There are a few things."

Mary took the list and looked it over. "Looks reasonable. Hmm, I'm not sure about scribblers. We've been using the slates. Scribblers have become an extravagance nowadays, but you'll need more wood for the stove soon enough."

She reached into her bag and pulled out a bottle of ink and a jar of flowers. "These will need some water." She strode over to the pail and added water to the jar. "I trust the children will mind you closely. If my lot are any trouble, make sure to tell me straight away."

"Will you tell me their names?" Emmy glanced at the row of children lined up behind their mother. She took up her pencil and added Florence, Arthur and Howard Drummond to her list.

By the time she said good day to Mrs. Drummond, it was 9:00. The school bell rang and Emmy hurried to the front door.

There was some scuffling to get through the small entryway. Emmy clapped her hands and directed the children to line up in an orderly fashion. The shelf of lunch pails was overflowing and so she cleared another shelf to hold the rest.

"Grade ones will take the first row," she said. "Then grade twos and grade threes can sit in the back." They were short quite a few desks. This had never happened at her school in Shelby.

"Miss, Miss! I haven't got a chair," said Cassie. Several other children flailed their hands in distress to tell her the same.

"You'll have to take a seat on the floor in front of the first row for now. We won't be at our desks for long."

A paper airplane whizzed above her head and Emmy reached out and caught it. She eyed some snickering boys in the back row. Her heart raced, watching them whisper to one another. The younger children watched with wide eyes. She must take control. Standing as tall as possible, she eyed each boy until the laughter subsided.

"That will be quite enough," she said crisply. The big boys stopped smiling. "You have wasted our limited resources and been disrespectful." Some of the boys sneered, but at least they stopped laughing.

She unfolded the paper and smoothed it out before her. "Still, it's quite good craftsmanship." The boys exchanged surprised looks. Emmy ignored the sweat that was trickling inside her dress. She knew she needed the oldest boys as allies.

"Please rise for God Save the King," she instructed. There was a clamour of feet and desks as the children rose. She stood close to the new students to demonstrate how to stand facing the framed picture of King George.

Most of the youngest children mumbled through the chorus, but Cassie, standing nearby, sang every word loud, clear and on key. They sang The Maple Leaf Forever and ended with The Lord's Prayer and The Ten Commandments.

"Please be seated," she said when they finished. "I am happy to meet you all. My name is Miss Bennett and I have come from Shelby to be your teacher."

"Will you be staying all year?" called out a boy whom she had not yet met.

"Please remember to raise your hand," Emmy demonstrated. "There are too many of you for me to hear all at once."

The little boy hung his head and his ears reddened. "Of course, you did not know this rule," Emmy continued. "It will be good for all of us to know this straight away." She took up her piece of chalk and wrote "Raise your hand" next to the number one.

"I will be staying on as your teacher for the year," Emmy answered his question. She noticed some girls whispering together in the middle of the classroom. "Rule number two in my classroom is that students are to look and listen when I am speaking." She watched the girls until they looked up at her. Then she wrote the second rule on the board.

"She started it!" piped up one of the girls with a long red braid and a lilting accent.

"The third rule is the Golden Rule," Emmy continued, ignoring the tattle. "Who can tell me what the Golden Rule is?" She raised her eyebrows and watched the sea of waving hands before her.

"Florence, please," she said.

"Do unto others what you would have them do unto you," she recited.

"Very good," said Emmy, copying the dictum onto the blackboard. "Now, who can tell me what this means?" She paused to choose a boy. "Samuel."

"It means we must treat everyone well," he said.

"Exactly," said Emmy. "We can practice this while everyone has the chance to tell me their names."

The children needed some reminders as everyone stated their names and she wrote them on the blackboard. She added another eleven students to her list and checked that she had the previous names correct. By the time this was finished, the youngest students were fidgeting.

"Grades three and up, collect your readers and study the first reading. Then, copy God Save the Queen onto your slates so I can assess your penmanship. I expect you to work studiously and quietly while I meet with grades one and two."

The younger children seemed pleased to have her full attention. She passed out their readers and had the grade two children pair up with the grade one children and read them a passage while she listened for a few minutes to each pair. One of the boys had considerable difficulty reading. Emmy noted he spoke only a few words of English. Two students seemed to be on track, but the rest would need a lot of work to get up to grade level. Emmy ignored a wave of despair.

"Please Miss, could I read some?" asked Cassie once all the grade 2 students had their chance.

"Certainly. If you would like to read, grade ones, you may now have a turn." Only Cassie was able to read more than a word or two, but Emmy made sure to praise each one for their efforts.

Emmy pointed to a list of words on the blackboard for the younger children to practice while she walked around the classroom to look over the copy work. She was impressed that most students seemed to be working quietly while she helped the younger children.

At recess break, Emmy took the time to pace the field with Bev so they could get to know their students better. Anne and Mel were nowhere to be seen.

"How does you class seem?" Bev asked.

"It will take some work, but they are a nice bunch. How about yours?"

"There certainly are a lot of them, but a few are keen to help me out."

One of the girls had a skipping rope and most of them congregated to play together. Some of the boys gathered to throw rocks at a can on the fence post, but she could not find the biggest boys.

"Georgia, where are your big brothers?" Emmy asked the oldest Blaine girl.

Georgia twisted her shoe in the dirt and nodded her head toward the barn.

"Thank you." Emmy marched toward the dilapidated building. Warm wind blew across the vast prairie, carrying the sound of hollering.

"Hellooo in here," she called after pulling the wide door open. Boys scurried past to hide in the corners. She remembered her brothers playing in the barn and knew it was probably best to leave them to it as much as possible.

"You may play in the barn as long as no one gets hurt. If I hear or see anything untoward happening in here, there will be a week-long suspension from the premises, do you understand?" No one called out their assent, but she saw some heads nodding in the corners. "Very well. Sam, I expect you to keep the boys in line."

"Yes Miss," said the boy from overhead.

"And I expect you to come running when I ring the bell." She closed the door and hoped her little speech would work.

She returned to the school room to post arithmetic questions on the blackboard. When the bell rang, she worked with the oldest children while the younger ones practiced their sums on slates. There was only one book of figures for the grade three students. She called out the problems while the students wrote them out on their slates. Tommy and Patsy proved quick with figures, so Emmy eventually gave them her job while she worked with the younger children. Sam seemed displeased that his younger brother should have a position over him, but he followed directions. She would have to be sure to give him a leadership position in another subject area.

It took some time to have the children wash hands before they ate their lunch. She would not have outbreaks of influenza in her classroom. She hadn't missed a whole month of school while her brother had mumps without learning the importance of good hygiene.

Emmy stifled a yawn after lunch and found a grade one student asleep at his desk. The first day of school was a long one, but she knew they would come to get used to the routine.

Emmy reached for the worn classroom globe and called for attention. "It's time for our Geography lesson," she said. Out of the corner of her eye, she noticed a small movement near her hand. She gasped and dropped the globe to the floor where it smashed.

"Oh no, miss!" Cassie said. "You'll get in trouble!"

Children began running up to see Emmy's mess and a little vole scurried between their feet and into a hidden corner of the room.

Emmy gathered her wits and knelt to clean up the broken globe. "I'm afraid the mice got to the globe before I wrecked it." She pointed out the large nest in the Atlantic Ocean. "I'm sorry I dropped it, but we couldn't have used it anyway. Patsy, will you get the broom?"

"What will you do with it?" Tommy asked.

"It's useless now. We'll have to throw it away."

"My dad won't like that one bit," Tommy shook his head. "We aren't supposed to waste anything."

"Then I'll send it home with you to be repaired," Emmy said, gritting her teeth.

It took some time to clean up the mess and settle the children back into their seats. She pointed out Canada and England on the well-used wall map and tried to use the apple Patsy had given her to demonstrate the shape of the world, but most of the children looked confused.

"What about Germany?" asked Robert after raising his hand and waiting his turn.

"Good question. It would be about here," she demonstrated. "We will create our own globe once I find an appropriate sphere," she said. "Does anyone have a pumpkin at home that they could bring to class tomorrow?"

Florence Drummond raised her hand and Emmy thanked her for the donation. "Make sure your folks approve."

Emmy left enough time at the end of the day for the children to do chores and play a game together. She had them sweep the floors, put away readers, clean slates and the chalkboard. She also sent the children to pour the wash water and drinking water onto the little Lilac bush struggling to grow in front of the school. She knew how important it was that the students see her as a harbinger of fun as well as rules. She set herself up as the finder in Hide and Seek and they played until she rang the bell, signalling it was time to go home.

A few mothers came early to peek into the class-room. Emmy rightly assumed they were new grade one parents, nervous about their children. She nodded at them but continued her game until the bell rang for the end of the day. Then she went to greet the mothers.

"I'm Ronald's mother," said a woman with a baby on her hip and worried eyes. "How did he do?"

"You've already taught him to write his name. He did very well," Emmy smiled and was pleased to see Ronald's mother relax.

"I'm Shirley's mother." Another woman held out her hand to Emmy.

"Oh yes. She had a little fall at lunch in the yard, but I think she's all better now." The little girl ran to grasp her mother's dress.

"This is Miss Bennett, mother," she said. "She gave me a cold compress for my scrape." She held out her knee for her mother's inspection.

Just then some older boys came racing out of the school house, whooping and hollering "No more teachers, no more books!" They nearly knocked Ronald's mother off balance.

"Boys!" said Emmy, but it was no use when she didn't know their names. She looked back to see if Anne or Mel were in sight to correct their students, but neither teacher came to the school yard. In fact, she hadn't seen either teacher since the smoky teacher's lounge. She and Bev ate their lunch to-gether in Bev's classroom, so they could keep an eye on the school yard.

"Are you all right?" Emmy asked the flustered mother. She nodded. "I'm sorry I can't do more. I haven't met those boys yet. I'll speak to their teacher."

"The big boys are scary," said Ronald. "I hope I never get to be so mean."

Emmy smiled at him and hoped the same thing.

# CHAPTER SIX

*Troubles*

Emmy sent the Blaine children home, so she could prepare for the next day when she saw Anne and Mel walking out of the school with their arms linked.

"Oh, I meant to speak to you about a couple of boys," Emmy said.

Anne gave Emmy a withering gaze. "Oh really? You ought to let us mind our own students and stay out of their way."

Anger flashed under Emmy's skin. "Well, I might if they didn't crash into the parents of my students."

Mel crossed her arms and glared. "So maybe you don't need to stand right in front of the school, taking up all the room."

"Listen here," Emmy's voice rose as if she were speaking to a misbehaving student. "I don't know who you worked with last year, but I will not be spoken to in such a manner. It is your responsibility to keep your students in hand." Emmy pointed at them as she spoke. "I will not stand to have the younger students bullied by older children who ought to know better."

Anne stepped closer to Mel. "You have no authority here, Miss Bennett. We're the senior teachers and we will not be instructed by you."

The two women linked arms again and marched away. Emmy was so shocked she could think of no way to reply.

"Oh my," said Bev, coming up behind Emmy. "That did not go well."

Emmy was shaking. "I have never met such obstinate people in my life. How on earth did they become teachers?"

"Come inside," Bev placed an arm around her shoulder. "We need to get ready for school tomorrow and then we can talk about what to do."

Emmy was grateful for her friend's calm support. Her hand still shook as she copied out the register alphabetically and went over her list of necessary supplies. Then she made out a schedule for the following day. On the three blackboards, she wrote out the reading, comprehension and spelling lessons for the next day. She would put up the arithmetic problems during recess just as her elementary teacher in Lester used to do.

Before leaving, she straightened desks and books and checked over her writing for errors. Then she and Bev locked the door and headed for their respective homes. Emmy couldn't help but be wistful when Bev turned toward the Fell's. She foresaw a dismal night with the Blaine's.

The rancid scent of burning vegetables reached Emmy long before she arrived at the farmhouse. The strains of a crying baby accompanied the charred scent. Her mood darkened. Why couldn't this woman manage her home? Emmy's mother had nine children and had dealt with the death of her first husband without this much fuss. Would poor food and neglected children be her lot for the next ten months?

Emmy checked her fiery emotions before she went inside. The smell was even worse. The baby was obviously ill and suffering from a complaint of the bowels. Millie looked pale herself and was clutching the wall with one hand and trying to soothe the baby at her hip with the other. Emmy's frustration melted.

"Take yourself off to bed," she said and took a stained apron from the hook. "I'm here now and I'll take care of the rest. I'll send Georgia to give you a hand with Baby."

In truth, she didn't know the baby's name. No one called him anything but Baby. She hoped it meant he would be the last for this already overcrowded family. She found Georgia outside and asked her to take the baby, so her mother could rest.

"I always take care of Baby. Why does it have to be me?" Georgia pouted. Her face was streaked with dirt. Emmy felt her irritation; being the oldest girl in a large family was a position she knew well.

"You're the most responsible." Emmy tried to bolster the girl's spirits. "Your mother is ill, and the boys haven't learned how to manage a baby. He's sick as well. He'll feel better if you're holding him."

"You're not my mother." Georgia gritted her teeth.

Emmy's tempter flared. "I'm your teacher and your elder. That's good enough."

Georgia's fists clenched, but she stomped to her mother's room to collect Baby.

Next, Emmy peeked in the pots and was tempted to throw the whole mess out for the chickens, but she well knew the scarcity of food. It was mainly the turnips that were burnt. She removed the pot from the stove, cut off the black bits and placed the remaining turnips on a plate while she scoured the pot. Hopefully, a mash would taste all right with a bit of salt and pepper.

There was a stew of cabbage, carrots and chicken. It tasted ghastly, but she forced herself to consider the horrid mouthful to ascertain what made it so bad. The cabbage was past its prime, the chicken was tough, and the carrots were undercooked. Mrs. Blaine must have cooked them in the wrong order. She rifled through the cupboard to check what was available. There was little to help, but she took a bottle of vinegar and a bit of cinnamon and then grabbed an apple from the surprisingly generous supply. She hoped salt and vinegar would soften the chicken and take away the bitterness of the cabbage. The apple and cinnamon would add sweetness. She added half a cup of water and set stew to simmer at a much lower heat.

Georgia arrived at her side, cradling Baby. "He's hot, Miss," she said, her eyes frightened.

"I'll get you a cloth and some water while you can unwrap him. He's lucky to have you." She smiled to reassure the girl. "You could sing to him." The baby had stopped howling but kept up a persistent whimper.

Shyness passed over Georgia's face, but when Emmy returned to the kitchen after finding a relatively clean cloth and a bowl of water, she heard Georgia softly singing Mary Had a Little Lamb to her brother. He grew quieter.

Emmy finished cooking and employed Cassie in setting the table. Mr. Blaine stepped in just as Emmy was about to call everyone to wash up. He surveyed the room and Emmy in an apron and a dark expression clouded his features.

"Where's my wife?" he growled and strode toward their bedroom.

"She's not feeling well." Emmy followed him. "She and the baby are both sick. She needs to rest." Her voice rose at the end as he placed his hand on her door knob.

Mr. Blaine turned and glared at Emmy, but he did not open the door. He turned to look at the baby in Georgia's arms.

"Please father, could you take him? I need to wash up," said Georgia.

Mr. Blaine took his son from his eldest daughter as if he weighed no more than a butterfly. He touched his lips to the boy's forehead and tucked the child more securely into his arms.

"She lost one before Johnny," he murmured. "I was worried."

Emmy rubbed her hands together. "I don't think it's anything serious, but likely quite contagious. It will be important for everyone to wash their hands frequently."

Mr. Blaine frowned at her. "You a nurse as well as a teacher?"

Emmy stood firm. "I'm a reader, sir and I had eight younger siblings myself. My mother was determined about washing hands after my father died so young. I follow her good example."

Mr. Blaine's features softened as his son fell asleep. "I'm sorry to hear about your father."

"Thank you," Emmy said before she returned to the kitchen to finish preparing dinner.

"Will you join us, Mr. Blaine?" she asked a few minutes later.

He shook his head. "I'll stay with my boy and help myself a little later. I should check on Millie as well."

Emmy nodded and returned to the kitchen to oversee the meal, making sure to set some aside for Mr. and Mrs. Blaine.

"I have some coal for the classroom," Florence Drummond said tentatively, holding an old pail at the door of the school the next morning. She was dressed in a clean but faded gingham dress and her long dark hair was carefully plated. She was holding an old pail.

"Come in," Emmy motioned to the stove and stepped forward to see what had been provided. Florence dumped the coal into the bucket by the stove. It was a tad chilly in the school, but the sun would warm the school later. They'd save the coal for colder days.

"Mother said she asked around, but there won't be any money for scribblers this term."

"Thank you, Florence. You've been very responsible. Would you please tell your mother we are short five desks?" Florence nodded and then Emmy ushered her out to play until the bell rang.

She had left the Blaine children to play in the yard. She wouldn't need as much help this morning. Out the school door, she noted the Blaine's had been joined by several other families. Dahlia Purdy trotted forward with an outstretched hand.

"Papa sent this," she said, slightly breathless.

Emmy took the proffered handkerchief and unwrapped several sticks of chalk.

"Very useful." She smiled at the freckled child, took the chalk and returned the handkerchief.

Dahlia would not take it. "Papa says you are to keep that as well. You may need it." She smiled and skipped away. Emmy turned over the piece of cloth. It was finely embroidered with the initials "PP" and neatly pressed. She guessed it had been saved since before the Great Depression when regular folks could afford finer materials.

Shortly, it was time to ring the bell and begin. The youngest children seemed proud to know what to do. They stood at attention to sing the morning songs and say prayers. Emmy assigned a different group of students to sit on the floor.

"Hopefully we'll have more desks soon," she reassured them.

"Can we play hide and seek today?" asked Howard after raising his hand and waiting his turn.

"Perhaps," Emmy said. "We must always do our work first and then see if there is time for play."

They began their lessons and she allowed herself a second or two of satisfaction that the children were already learning her routine. There was time at the end of the day for several rousing games of tag. She was pleased that she was able to catch Oscar Fleishman, one of the tallest boys in the class. He seemed equally as surprised.

"You're quite fast, Miss," he said breathing heavily.

Two parents were waiting at the door to speak to her.

"Hello Mrs. Drummond." She greeted Florence's mother. "Thank you for the coal."

"There should be more coming. I'll be reminding all the parents of their duty to heat the school. Don't be afraid to tell them yourself. Tom, you'll remember, I'm sure." She nodded at the other parent on the front step.

Tom was extremely thin with a bald patch taking over what remained of his wispy reddish hair. Freckles stood out from his cheeks and nose.

"We are short by five desks as well. The younger children have been taking turns sitting on the floor."

The heavy-set woman pursed her lips and shook her head. "I'm afraid you won't be getting any more desks. Miss Miller tried all last year, but there isn't enough money for more desks. We wrote to the other schools nearby, but they're short as well. Once harvest starts and the winter colds and flus, you won't have as many children as you do now. The desks should sort themselves out, likely by next week, wouldn't you say Mr. Purdy?" She gave a short laugh. "I hope my youngsters are behaving themselves?" She arched an eyebrow.

"Yes, very well." Emmy reassured her.

"I'll be off then," she said and called out to Florence, Arthur and Howard.

"Hello Mr. Purdy." Emmy held out her hand to greet the tall, quiet man.

"Hello Miss." he smiled and blushed.

"Thank you for the handkerchief and chalk." She remembered the gift Dahlia brought earlier.

"You're very welcome. Are my girls doing well?" He looked both uneasy and hopeful.

"Yes, sir."

He nodded several times, looked as if he wanted to say something, nodded once more and strode toward his daughters.

"Good day, Mr. Purdy," Emmy called after him.

Mrs. Blaine was pale and haggard when Emmy returned home. The children were scattered away from the house, except for Baby who slept in a basket on the table.

"How are you?" Emmy asked.

Mrs. Blaine opened her mouth to answer, but only sighed.

Emmy was tempted to escape to her room, but her conscience wouldn't allow it. "Would you like a cup of tea? Why don't you have a little rest and I'll boil the water."

A tear rolled down Mrs. Blaine's cheek. "Ain't no tea, Miss," she said. "I surely miss it."

"I've brought some," Emmy said. She hurried to her room, laid down her bag and coat and found the tin on her dresser. She would ask her mother for more in her next letter.

"It's become dreadfully expensive and hard to come by," Emmy said when she returned to the kitchen. "But my mother won't do without. No matter how little comes in each month, she finds enough for tea. I suppose that comes from being born in Scotland."

Mrs. Blaine hesitated before sitting at the table. The baby began to fuss, and her shoulders sagged, but she dutifully unwrapped him from his basket and put him to her breast.

"Where do your people come from?" Emmy asked once she'd put the water on the stove.

"Ireland," she replied.

"Then, we're neighbours," Emmy said. "We both

know the importance of tea."

She found the teapot, cups and saucers.

"It's been awful hard," Emmy almost missed Mrs. Blaine's whispered sentence. She froze as if she were seeing a baby deer in the bush. She didn't want to frighten her away. Then she proceeded to pour boiled water over the tea leaves as gently as possible.

"We were married in '27 and Frank had just started the farm. Things were starting to settle and we had our first three children, but the land turned on us. The dust storms, the heat, the grasshoppers . . . And our babies kept coming. We sold off what we could and then there was no one left with money to buy anything. . ." Her eyes were glazed, like an animal shortly before they died.

Emmy poured two cups of tea and brought them to the table. She hadn't been able to find any lemon. Her mother always used lemon in tea to keep the tea from staining her china cups. She could see the stains in Mrs. Blaine's cups. Clearly she wasn't worried about them.

"I took it all as best I could. We put cardboard in the children's shoes to make them last longer. We cut back our rations, lived on eggs and milk; fish when Frank had time to go fishing in the summer. But when my baby died, that was the end. . ." Her voice trailed off and her glassy eyes swam in tears.

Emmy wondered if she should reach out to pat this poor woman's hand, but she hardly knew her and didn't want to make her feel worse. The baby squirmed and she shifted him to her other breast.

Emmy took another sip of tea.

"Johnny will be the last baby," Mrs. Blaine looked down at her son. "I can't have any more. I'll make sure of it." There was something of steel hiding within this broken woman. She lifted her cup and closed her eyes as she inhaled the fragrant steam. "Thank you for the tea," she said. "I sorely needed it. And for your help last night. You shouldn't have to work in the kitchen after teaching all day."

"Think nothing of it," Emmy replied. "I'm used to working." She stood to survey the kitchen. "Is there something I can get started tonight?"

Mrs. Blaine's eyes flew open. "Oh no. Frank won't have it. I'll get to it in a minute. You're our guest."

Emmy imagined there'd been words between the couple. She struggled to keep her mouth closed. Mrs. Blaine's cooking was nearly inedible.

Emmy cleared away the tea things while her hostess rewrapped her baby and forced herself to her feet. At least she had a little colour in her cheeks.

# CHAPTER SEVEN

*News*

At the end of the week, Emmy was satisfied her class was beginning to understand the routines of the day. However, the noise level coming from Anne and Mel's classrooms was increasing. Emmy had learned to wait until the older students were dismissed before she allowed her own students to go. Bev did the same. They worried their smaller children would be bowled over by the bigger children racing through the hallway and out into the school yard.

Emmy supervised the school yard from the school steps as her students drifted home. Anne and Mel looked harried as they hurried out of the school together. "We have plans," Anne said as they breezed past. "Won't you two be dears lock up?" she waved her fingers at them. Her mood seemed to improve as she grew further from their classrooms.

"I wonder. . ." Emmy murmured.

"What?" asked Bev.

Emmy waited until the other teachers and all the students were out of view. Then she pulled Bev toward the upper classrooms. They stood at the doorway and surveyed the litter of papers, broken pencils and spitballs in Anne's room.

"How on earth?" asked Bev and Emmy pulled her to peer into Mel's classroom. It was marginally better, but still unkempt.

"I wonder what they do all day?" Bev mused.

"If they're this bad at the beginning of the year, just think what they'll be like in June." Emmy leaned on the door frame.

"Should we clean up?" Bev bit her lip.

"No. We can't say anything. We'll just have to let the school board see for themselves." She pulled out her key and locked the two classrooms.

"Do you think you can finish by five?" asked Bev.

"I'll try," Emmy replied and stretched her arms over her head. "I'm glad for the weekend."

"Me too," Bev said and disappeared into her organized classroom.


Emmy created her schedule for the following week, said goodbye to Bev and walked home. She had discovered Mr. Blaine was always out in the barn or on the field for at least an hour when she returned from school. She helped Mrs. Blaine start dinner with a few necessary suggestions on how best to cook their meagre meals without ruining the food. Then she would disappear into her room well before Mr. Blaine returned, none the wiser. Sometimes, she would sit in the tiny parlour holding Baby. Mr. Blaine and Baby seemed to approve of this situation and Emmy found him to be a rather sweet child. She well knew the plague of colic after helping care for so many younger siblings.

By the second week of school, there was no longer a lack of desks. Her students had many reasons for missing school including illness, helping at home and lack of transportation. Those who came regularly worked through their material with no trouble. Those who attended sporadically needed assistance when they returned. She didn't just have three grades to teach, but rather a different grade for nearly every student. She tried to make her lessons as broad as possible so that every child could learn something rather than having to teach thirty different lessons.

Emmy woke Sunday morning to loud wailing in their parlour. She sat up in alarm, thinking it was feral cats at first, but then realizing it was human.

She hurried into her dressing gown and stumbled into the parlour to find Mrs. Blaine clutching Baby and weeping on the worn sofa.

"Whatever is the matter?" Emmy asked, trying to see if Baby was okay.

"It's too cruel." Mrs. Blaine's face was splotched with red.

"What is too cruel?" Emmy said.

Mr. Blaine clenched his jaw and stared at the radio. "War has been declared," he said.

He stopped and stared at the radio and Emmy

sat on the other sofa as the children shuffled in, looking frightened. She'd never heard the radio played in the house before and had wondered how they could afford it when everything else was so sparse. The children began to whimper at the cold.

"Hush, now," Mr. Blaine said. "We can't hear the radio."

Music played from the box, but it was close to 7:00 and the news. They waited through two songs and Emmy wished for tea, but it didn't seem right to leave.

At seven, they heard it for themselves. "At 11:15 a.m. British time, Neville Chamberlain announced war with Germany," the broadcast began. Emmy and Georgia gasped while Mrs. Blaine resumed crying.

A crackling speech played next, a distant message from the British Prime Minister, Neville Chamberlain. "This morning the British Ambassador in Berlin handed the German Government a final note stating that, unless we heard from them by 11 o'clock that they were prepared at once to withdraw their troops from Poland, a state of war would exist between us.

"I have to tell you now that no such undertaking has been received, and that

consequently, this country is at war with Germany."

Mrs. Blaine's hand flew to her mouth.

"Oh dear," said Emmy, but could think of nothing else to say for several minutes.

"Frank," gasped Mrs. Blaine. "You'll have to go

to war." Her face was splotched with red and white patches and streaked tears.

"I'll do my duty," he said.

"My brothers," said Emmy. After several moments, she strode to the kitchen to start the stove. It was too much to take without the edifying powers of tea.

Pink, purple and golden flowers stood at attention in the bright autumn sun along the wooden sidewalk.

"I thought you might not come," Bev said as they walked together. "With the news of the war."

"I think church is for the best. We'll all be looking for some reassurance this morning. I hope Mel and Anne decide to come as well."

"Yes," agreed Bev.

Long before Bev and Emmy arrived at the solid country church, they saw its tall white steeple pointing to God. Emmy tried to direct her thoughts heavenward, but when they arrived, she knew she wasn't the only one who couldn't stop worrying about what was happening on earth.

"We already fought the Great War," said one of the women to a friend. Emmy recognized her as a mother from school.

"I will not allow my little Jack to fight in this war." Another mother clung to her son who wriggled to be let free. "I've already sacrificed a brother to this country." Tears shivered on her long black eyelashes.

Jack broke from his mother's grasp and raced toward the other boys who were creating a barricade of tumbleweeds in front of the church and racing around with pretend guns shouting "The Germans are coming. Quick! Protect the city!"

The church bell rang and Emmy and Bev queued to enter. Out of the corner of her eye Emmy noticed familiar lanky walk. Her eyes widened and her stomach fluttered.

"Looks like your fella can't stay away."

They found space in a back pew and were opening their hymn books when Lars slid beside them. Emmy smiled, but he only nodded. "What are you doing in Harding?" she whispered.

"I heard the news and I had to see you."

The organ started playing and the congregation rose, flipping hymnal pages. The pastor mustn't have had time to adjust his sermon.

"Not the best choice," Lars nodded at the title of the first hymn titled Welcome Happy Morning.

Bev shook her head. "It's a shame no one thought to change the hymns."

Few voices ventured to take on the happy song. When the minister opened his sermon with the phrase "God loves a cheerful giver", it was as if the entire congregation folded their arms and lowered their heads in shame. Could there be a more insensitive topic?

Fortunately, the minister realized their posture. "I do not know why God led me to this particular passage this week. It seems most inappropriate on this dark day." A few heads looked up.

"I pray that God would open our hearts to His word and trust that even though this seems the opposite of anything we want to hear, it is still the word of God."

Emmy had never heard such a remark in church. It seemed a humble thing for a preacher to say. She hoped, for everyone's sake, that Reverend Thomson was right.

After reading the passage of Scripture, Emmy was struck by the word "grace". Then the minister said, "Whether or not we are pacifists, we are called to give what God frees us to give. We will likely face considerable difficulties in the months ahead, but it remains that we must remember our Provider and to give back what is our due with thanksgiving."

It was a lofty thought, but Emmy felt her spirits lifted by the sentiment. It helped to think that God would give her the strength to face what was ahead.

Parishioners congregated on the grass in front of the wooden church after the service. People seemed to want to stick together. Emmy stood to the side with Lars.

"I'm planning to sign up, once Canada joins," he said after they watched the others in silence a few minutes.

Emmy leaned into him for support. He put an arm around her shoulders.

"Whoa there, Emmy. It's going to be okay."

She cleared her throat and stepped away from his grasp before anyone could see them. She placed a hand on her forehead.

"I have to," he whispered. "Earl's not fit for war. Someone needs to represent our family. How will I live with myself if I don't help my country?"

His eyes looked earnest, as if he was hoping she had an answer for him.

"Of course, you must," she said. "It just became too real when you said it. My brothers will have to go as well. It's our necessary sacrifice."

"I'll take you home." They moved away from the comforting crowd toward his horse.

"My mother is expecting me for lunch," Lars said once they were on their way. Emmy couldn't keep from sighing her disappointment.

"It's the worst timing, I know. I'd rather be with you." He reached out to take her hand.

"It can't be helped," Emmy said but she was comforted by his touch.

# CHAPTER EIGHT

*A Stiff Upper Lip*

On Sunday, September 10, Canada declared war on Germany. The next morning the school was filled with talk of whose father or brother would be enlisting. Emmy's lesson plans outlined a day of grammar, mathematics and reading comprehension, but the children shuffled in their seats, unable to concentrate. After saying their prayers and singing their morning songs, Emmy gave them their spelling words and announced they would be going on a scavenger hunt.

The children sat up, distracted from their worries and Emmy felt such an achievement was a worthy donation to the war effort.

"Bring your slates," she said. "We'll be looking for something that starts with each letter of the alphabet."

"Do we need to carry everything we find? What if it's a tree?" said Shirley, her brown braids quivering with excitement.

Emmy smiled. "No, just write the word the best you can. You can draw a picture if you like. We certainly can't carry a tree in our pockets."

They filed out of the classroom with slates and chalk. In the hallway, a great deal of racket spilled out of Anne and Mel's classrooms. When she glanced their way, she saw both teachers standing in the hallway with their backs against the classroom doors, gossiping.

"Good morning," Emmy said, hoping to embarrass them out of their poor teaching practice, but they only nodded and continued gabbing.

Outside, the air had warmed in the morning sun. Emmy pointed out a boundary for the children and told them to keep their voices low. Then she allowed them to wander in pairs and groups to hunt for the alphabet. The scent of cigarette smoke caught her attention and she followed the smell to the back of the school where she found two of Anne's students smoking behind the woodshed.

"Maria and Frances!" she whispered. She did not want the younger children to see.

"What?" said Frances with a stony stare while Maria tried to hide the cigarette behind her back.

"This is shocking behaviour." She saw Maria flick her cigarette behind her into dry kindling.

"Maria, pick that up!"

Both girls turned to see the cigarette catch and light on slivers of wood. Neither moved to stop the flame. Emmy pushed past them to stomp out the fire and stooped down to pick up the smoking cigarette.

"You can't prove that's ours," Frances said.

"I don't need to prove anything. I saw you with the cigarette and I will tell your parents."

"We just found it here," said Maria. "I think it's Miss Miller's. We see her smoking here all the time."

"Yes, you should be yelling at her," said Frances.

"Stop lying and get back to class. You can be sure I'll tell your teacher and your parents everything I've seen. There will be consequences," Emmy said, but her confidence wavered. The girls probably had seen their teacher smoking behind the school.

Maria and Frances glared at Emmy, but obeyed her orders and, with heads pressed together in barely hushed outrage, they marched back to school. Emmy held the cigarette between her fingers. She hated to let the little ones see her with the offending object, but she must not lose the evidence and dare not lay it down. She searched the ground and found a discarded matchbox, more proof the girls had seen their teacher smoking. She made sure the cigarette was no longer burning before she stuffed it into the box and hid it in her skirt pocket. The scent lingered on her fingers. She strode toward the water pump to rinse them.

Fortunately, her students were too engrossed in their task to have noticed the little drama and Emmy had a few minutes to calm her thumping heart.

Once the children went out for recess, Emmy stormed into the staff room while Bev watched the school yard.

"Anne, I have something to tell you," she said, then coughed and tried to wave away the blue smoke that clung to the stuffy air.

"How do you know I care to hear it?" Anne said through pursed lips.

Emmy ignored her insolence and continued. "I caught Maria and Frances smoking in the woodshed. They said it was your cigarette they found." She pulled the offending item from her pocket.

Mel's eyes were round with worry and she studied her friend.

"Little snots," Anne took another drag of smoke before reaching out to take the matchbox. "I'll give them each the strap and send them home. I'll be glad to be rid of them for the rest of the day."

Emmy ground her hands into her hips in frustration, but she could do nothing more. She must accept her colleague's punishment and hope the girls' parents were astute enough to ask more probing questions.

Despite the enormous changes occurring in their country and around the world, the life of the school carried on. The children were unsettled, but Emmy's students were young enough to be distracted by games and various contests and competitions.

Anne and Mel's classes continued to disintegrate and sometimes she overhead them saying "Emmy and Bev have such easy classes. If only they knew how hard we work." It made Emmy's blood boil. She hoped for changes in the upcoming school board meeting.

The first board meeting of the year was scheduled for the last Friday of September. Emmy and Bev whispered together as they prepared for school that morning.

"Is there anything we can say about the upper grades?" Bev said as she wrote up her morning reading on the blackboard.

"I don't see how. We need to bide our time. I'm sure the children have told their parents what's happening in their classrooms." Emmy was checking over her stockings. She'd already put her finger through one that morning. It wouldn't do to appear before the board with runs.

Bev let out an exasperated puff of air and slammed the chalk onto the chalk holder, breaking it in two. "I just can't stand that our school sounds like a circus."

"Let me help." Emmy reached out to take the larger piece of chalk and finish writing the sentence.

Bev smiled. "Your penmanship is so much nicer than mine. The children will wonder who wrote this. I'm sorry, I am so worried about the school board meeting."

Emmy surveyed Bev and noted a piece of hair bobbing where it shouldn't. She popped a pin into place. Bev's hair was back in control. "You have nothing to worry about. You're a wonderful teacher."

Bev patted her hair and hugged her friend. "I can't imagine teaching with Mel and Anne without you."

Once Emmy had gotten through reading and arithmetic, she announced the Board Meeting to her class. "We're having special guests at the school house tonight. We want our classroom to look its very best."

The children seemed pleased to help and some of the girls offered to gather wildflowers to brighten the classroom. Emmy allowed Shirley, who was the best at drawing, to decorate the blackboard with a fall scene. She thanked her class for their keen effort as they filed out the door.

Then she let them out to play their newest game craze, Anti-I-Over, using the school barn as the divider. She joined the worst team to help make them fair.

"Anti-I-Over!" called the other team, tossing the ball blindly over the barn. At that moment, Cassie ran to Emmy to show her a purple coneflower. Emmy leaned over to look just as the ball came down on her face. It catapulted her glasses to the ground and she heard a despairing crack.

"Oh no, Miss Bennett!" Cassie bent to pick up the spectacles. "They're broke."

Emmy did not bother to correct her grammar. Her spirits sunk. She was helpless without her glasses. Cassie handed them over and Emmy held them close to her eyes to assess the damage. The left arm bent at a crazy angle. She removed herself from the game to see if there was anything to be done.

"It's three o-clock," announced Georgia Blaine.

"Can I ring the bell, Miss?"

Emmy nodded and held her glasses to her face to make sure all the children left safely.

Emmy wished she could present tea and cookies to the board, but she had neither the means nor the time for such extravagance. It was difficult to get anything done when she needed one hand to hold her glasses in place at all times. Fortunately, Mary Drummond arrived with a thermos of coffee, several mugs and a basket of fresh-baked scones.

"Looks fine in here," Mary nodded her approval.

"Thank you," Emmy felt better about her preparations.

Mary lowered her voice and checked the room for any eavesdroppers. "Of course, it is actually my husband who is on the board, women not being allowed." She arched an eyebrow as if daring Emmy to say something. Emmy smiled and Mary took it for acceptance.

"However, my husband is too busy to attend meetings. Usually both spouses are meant to come, but you'll find Mrs. Blaine is never well enough, Lord bless her, with all those children to take care of. And, of course, Mrs. Purdy passed on many years ago, so it's usually Mr. Fell, Mr. Blaine, Mr. Purdy and me."

"I'll be happy to have you here," Emmy said.

"Very good," Mary said. "We'll be starting with the upper grades today. Your class will be last."

By the time the board members came to her room, Emmy had planned her entire week and the week after, though she wondered at the quality of the plan when her mind kept drifting elsewhere. She checked her pocket mirror again to make sure her hair was in place and stood to receive them.

"Thank you for waiting, Miss Bennett," said Mrs. Drummond. "I'm sure it's been a rather long day."

Mr. Purdy reddened when he shook Emmy's hand. They pulled out a few adult-sized chairs from storage, creating a semi-circle at the back of the classroom with the coffee and baking set on the nearest shelf, accompanied by a jar of prairie wildflowers. Finally, Mr. Blaine arrived to fill out the circle of four.

"Best get started," he said after removing his hat and perching on the empty chair.

"Let's begin by officially welcoming Miss Bennett," Mary said, looking down at her notes. "She seems to be doing a fine job. My Florence likes her and say she is firm but kind." She smiled at Emmy who returned the favour.

"We didn't have fun in my day like they do with Miss Bennett," Mr. Blaine sniffed. "Are you sure they'll get through all of their studies?"

Emmy felt as if she'd been slapped, but she swallowed the offence and answered his question.

"I have a copy of my year-long plans," Emmy shuffled through the papers she'd prepared. "We are perfectly on target for completing all necessary requirements for the year, if the children attend classes." Mr. Blaine had kept his oldest two sons home the past week and a half. Mary Drummond took furious notes and Mr. Purdy cleared his throat.

Mr. Blaine exhaled sharply. "I don't know how things were run in Shelby, but in Harding, teachers are expected to plan for harvest. You need to work ahead, expecting that children will be missing from school now and then. If we don't get the harvest in, there won't be any money to run the school." Red was creeping up his neck.

Emmy bit her lip and looked from Mary to Mr. Fell to Mr. Purdy for help, but they would not meet her eye. "Thank you, sir," she said at last. "I will keep that in mind." But she said it through clenched teeth. She knew from years of living with her step-father when to concede in battle.

Mary Drummond sat up taller. "Thank you, Mr. Blaine and Miss Bennett. Next in business is the first school social."

Mr. Blaine harrumphed.

"I don't know if you are aware, Miss Bennett, that our school teachers are expected to host bimonthly socials. They are fundraisers for the school and occasionally for other community projects."

"Yes, we had a similar practice in Shelby," Emmy said.

"Excellent," Mary examined her notes. "The first will be held on October 7th. It's a Friday night. Your room is used for all socials. You can have the children assist you in preparing the classroom. Desks must be pushed to the side. You may decorate much as you have tonight," she motioned a hand around the room. "It's the Thanksgiving weekend, so you may want to add a cornucopia. I'll approach parents for decorating materials. They will also bring food for a lunch as well as beverages."

"There's no alcohol, Miss Bennett," said Mr. Purdy timidly. "Of that, you can be reassured."

"Our community also accepts dancing," Mary studied Emmy. Emmy nodded her acceptance.

"Good. So, that's all settled. We appreciate your help."

"Is it wise to go on with the dance, Mrs. Drummond, when our country is at war?" Mr. Blaine said, his eyes steely.

"I've always felt it best to keep spirits up during difficult times," Mrs. Drummond replied, her steel was on display in her voice.

"Purdy, doesn't it all seem like a waste of time?" Mr. Blaine tried the other board member.

Mr. Purdy looked down at his fingernails, inspecting them closely. "It may be a bit early to tell. We could wait and see how many sign up and ask some of the members of the community."

"That sounds very wise," Mr. Fell cut in. "In the mean time, we'll carry on with our plans.

Emmy was given a few minutes to share any needs in the classroom. She brought up scribblers, pens, ink and desks as necessities, but was given little hope of their provision.

"Times have been difficult here," Mr. Fell said. "I hope you'll understand."

Emmy, of course, was well aware of this fact. She had agreed to take the teaching post for minimal pay with room and board. She cleared her throat.

"I have a more personal request." She removed the glasses she'd been holding in place. "I am very near-sighted and today my glasses were broken while I played with the children."

Mr. Blaine harrumphed again and Emmy felt the sting to her pride.

"I need my glasses in order to teach." She gazed down at the broken spectacles. "I have not yet received any wages in order to fix them."

"Oh dear," murmured Mr. Purdy.

The three board members exchanged looks for a minute.

"I'm afraid we haven't dealt with such a request before," said Mrs. Drummond. "Emmy, do you mind if we take a few minutes to discuss the matter?"

Emmy agreed. "It only just happened this afternoon."

She let herself outside of the school, closing the door behind her. The wind had grown cold and she wrapped an arm around her body to fight off the chill. She needed the other arm to hold her glasses in place. She had an odd desire to cry. She never allowed herself to cry, but she felt the school board blamed her for her broken glasses or perhaps for her myopic vision itself. Had they never broken something they needed?

Just as she was beginning to hear her step-father's voice again and again, chiding her on her clumsiness and worthlessness, Mary Drummond stepped out on the porch.

"Oh my, it has gotten chilly," she wrapped a plump arm around Emmy's shoulders and led her back inside. "I think you'll be pleased with the decision." She was smiling, a dimple in each cheek and the ghostly voice of Emmy's stepfather dissipated.

"Miss Bennett," began Mr. Blaine while looking down at some papers before him. "Unfortunately, you have entered the teaching profession at a time when most people are barely surviving on the prairies. We hope things will improve by June, but at this time, we are not able to pay your salary."

Emmy's heart thumped painfully in her chest. She felt like Mr. Blaine was mocking her for thinking she deserved to be paid for her work.

"However, we realize we must assist you with your glasses. You clearly can't be expected to teach without them. We hope you will be more careful in your teaching duties." He looked up from his papers then, directly into her eyes. Emmy reddened with rage and shame.

"We have decided to give you the full amount required to mend your glasses."

Her face was frozen and must look unappreciative, so she made herself smile. "Thank you." She hated the thought of being a charity case.

"I will take you to town this weekend to have them repaired," said Mrs. Drummond. "Best to bring a list along. I'm sure there are other things you require."

# CHAPTER NINE

*Going to Town*

Emmy settled into her room to finish writing a letter for her mother and siblings. It had grown quite thick. Fortunately, her mother had sent along a good supply of postage. Once she signed off, she carefully placed her damaged glasses on her wobbly dresser and blew out the candle. She was beyond tired after her week at school, the ordeal over her glasses, and her first Board meeting.

Emmy woke early to prepare for her trip to town. She helped Mrs. Blaine make breakfast and was drying the dishes when Mary Drummond knocked on the door.

"Helloo!" Mary hollered into the tiny kitchen. Emmy was pleased she'd had time to put the kitchen into order.

"Would you like a cup of tea before we go?" she said.

"No thank you. I've taken mine at home. We'd best be off. I've got Florence in the buggy with her birthday money burning a hole in her pocket." Mary's bubbly energy was a nice contrast to the starkness at the Blaine household.

Emmy set her glasses down to put on her coat and hat. Then she held them in place with one hand while clutching her hand bag in the other.

"You're lucky you broke them the day before a weekend. I don't know how you would have managed your glasses and your classroom if you'd broken them on a Monday." Mary clucked her tongue and shook her head. "God's providence, I'd say."

Emmy mused how God's providence was allowed when things worked out, but never blamed for years of bad crops, grasshoppers and gophers.

Mary's driving, like her personality, came in bursts of energy followed by long lags of slow pacing. The horses pulling the buggy were lazy unless prompted. Then they grew overly excited and went too fast. Emmy held so tightly to her glasses that her fingers grew numb.

"What are you planning to buy with your birthday money, Florence?" Emmy asked during a slower part of the ride.

Florence sighed. "I was hoping to have enough for the Shirley Temple doll at the General Store. I don't think I do and I wonder if it's still there. If not, I might think about some sweets or a new pair of gloves."

"Shirley Temple's lovely, isn't she? I wonder if she has time for school with all her filming?" Emmy said.

"She's eleven this year," said Florence.

"Is that so?" Emmy said. "I suppose I always think of her as she was in her first films, when she was no more than a baby."

"She going to be in one of the Mountie movies soon," Florence said. "I read about it in a magazine."

The Drummonds must have more money than the average family in Harding to buy magazines. The last magazine Emmy read had been at least two years old, passed down from house to house in Shelby. There were no magazines or even papers at the Blaine house.

"Well, I hope you can buy your doll," Emmy said. "That would be a very nice gift."

"I'm lucky not to have any sisters to share with," Florence said, but then she coloured. "Not that I mind sharing, Miss Bennett. It just seems like the Hamm and Purdy girls have nothing to call their own."

Emmy chuckled. She knew the sentiment well. "Don't your brothers get into your things?"

Florence shook her head. "Oh no, Arthur and Howard are good brothers. Perhaps it's because I'm so much older than they are, but they mind me very well. I play games with them in return."

"Don't believe her for a second, Miss," cackled Mary. "Just this morning, she was hollering at them something fierce!"

"Mama!" Florence blushed. "I had to. They were

roughhousing and about to break something."

Mary put a thick arm around her thin daughter. "I'm only teasing, my love. You're like a second mother to our boys. I'm grateful for you."

Emmy felt a stab of discomfort over the easy affection between mother and daughter. Perhaps it was the way of a smaller family. There didn't seem to be enough affection to go around in her larger family. Maybe if her own father were still alive. . .

Thirty minutes later, they arrived in town. They passed the tall, sun-bleached grain elevator, surrounded by farmers bringing in their harvests. Then they came to the long dusty main street lined with the post office, general store, gas station, hotel and repair shop.

"We'll start with your spectacles," said Mary. "You've endured long enough." They stepped into the little shop, ringing a bell as they entered. There was already a line-up of men and women waiting to have things repaired. Emmy snuck a peek at Florence who looked like she was about to burst with impatience.

"Go on ahead," Emmy said, joining the queue. "We can meet at the Post Office."

They agreed on a time and Florence skipped off, holding her mother's hand and chattering away. Mary tossed Emmy a grateful smile.

Ahead of Emmy was a man with a broken scythe, and a boy with his father holding a broken wagon. She noticed the repairman was careful and thorough. She'd worried he might be more concerned with being quick than being good, but that wasn't the case. When her time came, she showed him the break and he asked her to put the glasses on and take them off a few times to be sure.

"Shouldn't be but a few minutes, love," he said in a Scottish brogue that reminded her of her mother's. They used to tease her about it, but she'd only smiled.

Emmy was nearly blind without her glasses. She tried not to show the panic she felt when all she could see were fuzzy shapes, but suddenly there was a man at her arm, speaking to her.

"Hello Miss." It looked like he touched the brim of his hat to her. "Beautiful morning."

"Hello," she said.

"I need this pitch fork soldered, Mac," he turned away from her. "Can I leave it with you and come back tomorrow? Don't have much time today." There was something familiar about his voice.

"Sure thing, Al," the repairman said.

"Though I wouldn't mind spending more time with you, ma'am," he touched his hat again and disappeared before Emmy had a chance to see him with her glasses on. It made her feel small and vulnerable. She tapped her foot.

"Don't mind him," said the repairman. "He isn't any harm. Al Purdy. Has a couple of daughters. His wife died a few years ago."

"Mr. Purdy?" she said.

"You know him? You must need these glasses pretty badly. Almost done now."

A few minutes later, her glasses were repaired. Emmy put them on and felt her confidence and determination return.

"Perfect!" said Mac.

She counted out the money Mary had given her for the task and was pleased to have some change to return.

After meeting at the Post Office, Mary insisted on buying lunch for them all at the Café. "Your terms were Room and Board," she said. "So, all your meals are included."

Her own family never bought lunch in town. Mary recommended the oxtail soup and Emmy found it tasty, though nothing like her mother's cooking. She felt an ache for home but pushed it away.

Florence did not have enough money for the coveted Shirley Temple doll, but she chatted on about how pretty it looked and what she wore. She was contented with her bagful of penny candies. Emmy wished she'd recognized Mr. Purdy without her glasses on. It felt like he'd seen her naked and hadn't even bothered to introduce himself.

Chapter Ten: School Dance

Only two men from the small community of Harding had signed up for the war effort. There was lots of talk of conscription, but the government seemed wary of forcing men to enlist. especially after the last war. It was decided that the School Dance would go on as planned, with some of the money being donated to the war effort.

The following week at school, Emmy began

planning the dance. The children made turkeys and leaves out of the small supply of paper. She asked them to bring any used newspapers, cloth or magazines they could find at home to make a little scarecrow in one corner. She also found a ragged cornucopia basket in the small storage room and the children brought a small selection of pumpkin and zucchini to add some colour. She supposed they could only be thankful for what was given.

Emmy enjoyed organizing the party. Some of girls stayed after school with Emmy and Bev to learn how to crochet. Fortunately, she and Bev could make five doilies as fast as the little girls could produce one, but they made enough to decorate the long tables for night lunch. The children memorized autumn poems from their readers including her favourite, Autumn Fires, by Robert Louis Stevenson:

> *In the other gardens*
> *And all up the vale,*
> *From the autumn bonfires*
> *See the smoke trail!*
>
> *Pleasant summer over*
> *And all the summer flowers,*
> *The red fire blazes,*
> *The grey smoke towers.*
>
> *Sing a song of seasons!*
> *Something bright in all!*
> *Flowers in the summer,*
> *Fires in the fall!*

She recited the poem as she walked to and from school in the crisp fall air. The children also learned songs and a short play about Thanksgiving to present at the dance.

On Friday night, she, Bev and some of the town children stayed late to move desks to the side, place doilies on the tables and decorate the blackboards with Thanksgiving drawings. All that was left was to arrive early and start the fire.

Emmy wore her best dress. She had only two; one for everyday and one for church. Her best dress was refashioned from one of her mother's. Even though it was old and meant for a married woman, Emmy liked the frill at the neck and the way the flowery fabric flared on her calves. Fortunately, she still had some good stockings, although she was beginning to wonder if she would ever be able to afford more.

Emmy left early, carrying a basket of scones she had baked. She wore her warmest coat and wrapped her scarf around her hair, hoping her curls would hold against the stiff wind. She strode briskly to fight the chill and was soon warmed by the journey.

The fields surrounding her were dry and brittle. Some were abandoned, she knew, by farmers who hadn't survived the long dry spell. She wondered where they were now, their boarded-up houses left to alternately bake and freeze on the prairies.

She saw Mr. Purdy waiting at the door with a fistful of orange Marigolds.

"Mr. Purdy," she smiled, trying to ease his obvious discomfort. "Those will liven up the school room. Thank you."

She unlocked the door while Mr. Purdy shuffled off the stoop to the ground, giving her an advantage of height.

"I came to see if you needed any help," he stammered when she had the door open and was about to step inside.

"That's very kind. Would you tend the fire? I'll find a jar for the flowers."

He looked relieved to be given a job. Emmy placed the Marigolds on the welcome table, lit the lamps, and the school slowly grew warm from the coal stove.

"Thank you, Mr. Purdy. You've given me the gift of time," Emmy said while she arranged her scones on a flowered plate.

Mr. Purdy grimaced and Emmy tried to follow his distant gaze. "Is something the matter? You look disturbed."

He cleared his throat several times, turned as if to leave and then changed directions abruptly. "Would you care to dance with me this evening?" he said in a low, formal voice.

Emmy fought the urge to laugh. "I'm fond of square dancing. How about the first one?"

Mr. Purdy nodded, but did not smile. "I need to gather Dahlia and Rosemond. They should be ready by now." He turned and left.

So that was why he blushed whenever he saw her. Well, she'd be careful. She had signed a contract promising not to get married while teaching at the school and he was a widower. Not to mention Lars...

Parents and children arrived in their finest, carrying the best cakes and sandwiches they could muster. Emmy and Bev stood at the beverage table, ladling out punch. They almost didn't recognize some of the boys.

"Hello Miss Bennett," said Oscar, who towered over her in an oversized suit. His dark hair was slicked to the side.

"You look well," she greeted him.

"Well enough to dance with?" His face turned deep red and he looked over his shoulder at a line-up of snickering boys. He must have been dared.

"I suppose," Emmy raised an eyebrow, wondering if he'd accept the challenge.

Oscar swallowed and nodded once before scurrying over to join his friends.

The band of fiddlers in the corner suddenly broke into a cacophony of tuning and children began running around the school-house. She was about to tell the children to settle down, when a hush fell over the room. Mr. Blaine stepped in front of the musicians who let their instruments rest.

"Welcome one and all to our Thanksgiving Dance," he said, his voice a low baritone. The crowd applauded.

"Thank you to our teachers, Miss Bennett, Miss Lafferty, Miss Miller and Miss Flemming for organizing the school room." He gestured toward them all. The crowd clapped again. Emmy tried not to scowl at the thanks. Anne and Mel hadn't lifted a finger to help with the evening, but they were accepting their praise with modest-looking smiles.

"A reminder that there is absolutely no tolerance for drinking or roughhousing. This is a family event and we expect proper behaviour. Without further ado, let us welcome the Harding Fiddlers."

Parents and students either formed partners to dance or moved to the side. Mr. Purdy claimed Emmy and they joined a square. The fiddlers set their bows in position and Mary Drummond's husband stepped forward as the caller.

They played Turkey in the Straw and Mr. Drummond made a sport of trying to confuse the dancers by calling out strange formations and leaving them to the last minute before he told them the next. The room filled with laughter and sweaty couples. The older boys propped open windows and doors to cool down the school room. Oscar arrived at her side the minute Turkey in the Straw was over. Mr. Purdy bowed but Emmy avoided his pathetic eyes. She danced with Oscar through Oh Susanna before she begged for a drink of punch.

"You'd better have a big drink, Miss," Oscar advised. "You dance well and there'll be plenty more gents wanting a dance."

Emmy shook her head at his cheek but took his advice. She noticed Mr. Purdy trying to find her in the crowd and purposely moved further away. She had no intention of encouraging him. She spotted Mrs. Drummond and marched toward her.

"Good evening Miss Bennett. Don't you look

lovely," Mrs. Drummond was stuffed into a dress several sizes too small.

"Thank you," Emmy said.

"It's a good turnout. Should raise enough funds for those scribblers you mentioned," Mary took a dainty bite from a plateful of home baking. "I'm afraid most of it will go toward fuel for the stove, however. Usually does."

Mary looked about her as if trying to measure if someone could overhear. "You'd be wise to keep your distance from Mr. Purdy. He's been mighty lonely."

"Yes, thank you," Emmy pursed her lips.

"You're a fine dancer," Mrs. Drummond's voice returned to a regular volume. "I never could do the steps fast enough." She laughed at her deficiency. Mr. Purdy was moving toward them. Mary winked at Emmy.

"Ah, Mr. Purdy, I wanted your advice on something." Mary took his arm and led him in the opposite direction.

After several more dances, Emmy prepared the children for the Thanksgiving program. She gathered them near the chalkboard and when the musicians took a break, they recited poems, sang songs and put on a short play about Thanksgiving. For the most part, parents looked on with pride and clapped for every effort. Mr. Blaine; however, seemed to be glowering from his place by the wall. She wondered how the program had offended him or if was just his general disdain for her.

After the program, there was night lunch. Emmy

was amazed at the bounty in spite of another hard year. She treated herself to pinwheel cookies, egg salad sandwiches, tea and cake. She was growing a bit drowsy when the music started up again and she was caught unawares by Mr. Purdy for a third dance.

Fortunately, it was so lively and energetic that Mr. Purdy couldn't divulge the secret that seemed to seep from his pores. She excused herself immediately afterward and kept her distance for the remainder of the night.

The children grew tired and ornery by midnight, and their parents finally dragged them home. The men helped move the desks back into position and Emmy and Bev organized the older children to sweep the floors and wipe the tables. Anne and Mel had already left. Finally, at 1 a.m., Emmy and Bev locked up the school. Mr. Blaine had left long ago and after she said goodnight to Bev, she was glad to have some time to herself to contemplate the success of her first school function and a bright moon to guide her back to the farm.

# CHAPTER TEN

*Frightening Tales*

Monday, the students were subdued after their late night at the school dance. Emmy herself was low on energy. She focused on math and spelling drills for the morning and read stories by the fire after lunch. Normally, she would have let the children out early to play in the school yard, but it was too windy and dusty. By the end of the school day, it was already dark.

"Please Miss," said Cassie. "Won't you walk home with us? I'm afraid."

Emmy agreed and hurried to copy out Tuesday's lessons on the blackboard. More parents arrived with horses and buggies than usual, but Mr. Blaine was not among the cautious.

She and the Blaine children stayed close while the wind whipped around them. Even the oldest boys, who usually ran ahead, needed no urging to stick together. Dry dirt drove into their eyes and noses.

"Why don't we run a while?" Emmy yelled to be heard over the wind. She hoped they took it as a challenge rather than the dreadful worry it was. The children ran without comment while Emmy watched the skies for twisters.

Cassie was the first to get a cramp and they slowed and encouraged her to keep going.

"I want to keep running, but I can't," Cassie said, tears streaming down her cheeks.

"Don't worry, sis," Sam said with a soft punch to his sister's arm. "You aren't much faster running than you are walking."

"Stay close together and I'll tell you a story," Emmy said.

The children gathered together while the dirt drove like needles into their faces. Emmy showed Cassie how to shield her eyes.

"I was fifteen when my little sister and I were caught in a dust storm. Just like you, we were walking home from school." Emmy glanced up at the sky.

"It was even darker than it is today. Suddenly, we saw a patch of earth twisted into the air. I pulled Becky to my side and covered her face with my handkerchief. I told her she had to follow me like we were playing Blind Man's Bluff. If she didn't lose me, we'd win."

"That's a clever idea," Katherine said.

"She followed me as I led her away from the great dark cloud. Just before it was about to swallow us, I saw a farm ahead. I memorized the location and led us through whipping clods of dirt until we made it to the front step. I banged on the door.

"Did they let you in?" said Tommy.

"Not at first. They thought it was just more wind banging on the door and screaming, but then they could make out my words."

"What did you say?" said Cassie.

"It's Emmy and Becky Bennett. Please let us in! Then they opened the door and pulled us inside. We stayed the night."

"Were your parents worried?"

Emmy remembered her step-father's angry face the next day, her mother's wringing hands. "I expect they were. But there was nothing they could do until we made it home."

"There aren't any houses between school and our home," Georgia said, her eyes round.

Emmy checked the sky. "This storm isn't as bad. We'll make it."

They pushed on together, taking turns leading one another as the "blind man".

At last, they arrived at the farm.

Mrs. Blaine stood at the window, her face pale. Emmy tried to calm the tremor of rage she felt for Mr. Blaine before she went inside.

"You made it," Millie said, touching each of her children as they entered. "I was so worried. It's too dark."

"Where's Daddy?" Cassie said.

Mrs. Blaine pursed her lips. "He's in the barn. He'll be expecting Sam and Tommy to help. You're late today."

"They waited to go with me," Emmy said. "I

thought it was wise, considering the storm." She squeezed her hands into fists, fighting the urge to yell.

"Thank you," Mrs. Blaine said. "Tommy, try to explain things to your father."

Emmy excused herself from the kitchen to work in her bedroom. She was shaking and needed to be alone.

Emmy was the oldest surviving child in her family. She'd had an older brother, but he died when she was only three. Her father had passed away two years earlier. As the oldest child and the only stepchild, she knew what it was to live with unreasonable expectations.

"Your mother is ill," her stepfather told her when she was five. "You will be expected to take over the washing and cleaning. No mistakes!"

She'd stomped her feet in protest, but this was met with a quick reproof. She learned to hold her tongue.

If she'd left a spot on the dishes or a streak on a glass, he would make her do them all over again. Her mother had seven more children and the dishes piled up.

"Your brother has the measles," her stepfather told her when she was seven. "You'll have to stay home from school to help. They'll be worried about you spreading the disease."

She had nursed three siblings through the measles but managed to fend off the disease herself.

She'd missed three months of school, right at the beginning of the year when everything was fresh. It had taken her two years to catch up.

"You can't go to high school, Emmy," her stepfather had announced at the end of grade eight. "Your mother needs you at home and there's no money besides."

She smiled grimly at the memory. She had worked behind his back to fight that pronouncement. She wrote letters to her cousin who lived in the town where the high school was. They loved Emmy and agreed to provide her free room and board while she attended school.

"One less mouth to feed," she'd whispered to her stepfather. She watched her words have their calculated effect. She left it at that and within three days, he agreed to let her go.

Yes, she knew what it was to have an unreasonable father, but it still took every effort to fight her temper and hold her tongue. She would never marry such an unfair man.


Emmy did her best to catch up the children on their school work after the big dance. Many students were missing with the late harvest and an outbreak of the flu. To encourage attendance, she turned her lessons to Halloween themes.

"Miss Bennett, please tell us a spooky story," said Bertie after lunch recess on a crisp day.

The school readers had no such stories. There were fairy tales and poems about the seasons, but the publishers must have thought it best not tell children anything frightening. Emmy was not as fastidious.

"I will, but then I expect you to write one of your own," she said and gathered the children on the floor in front of the stove. Even the oldest students looked like little children when they gathered to hear a story.

"There once was a poor old woman who lived in the deep dark woods with her two beautiful daughters," she began and nearly slipped into her Mother's Scottish brogue. "The mother was sick and eventually took to her bed for she was too weak to do even the simplest chores.

"That's so sad," said Rosemond.

Emily fell into the magic of the story through the expression on her students' faces. She found herself adding details to the character's poverty and desperation to draw in the children. Cassie and Rosemond held hands in fear.

"Mary hurried on with a watchful eye until she came to a little clearing where a tiny house stood in a ray of sunshine. She knocked on the door and called 'Hello, I'm Mary, I am looking for work. Is anyone home?'

"No one replied, but the door creaked open. Mary had been walking a long time and was tired and hungry, so she let herself in and took a draught of water.

"The inside of the cottage was in complete disarray. After a mouthful of bread, she took off her cloak and put on her apron, setting to work. She made seven untidy beds, piled seven spoons and bowls in the sink to wash, dusted the furniture and then swept the floor, making sure to get every nook and cranny and to sweep under the rug. Perhaps if she did a good job, whoever lived in this place would be willing to pay her to come back.

"Just as she finished and looked about the room to survey her work, she heard the sound of feet stomping up to the door. She froze, worried they might be angry with her for coming inside. The door creaked on its hinges while Mary trembled." Emmy drew out the words and paused to allow the children to imagine who was behind the door. Then she lowered her voice dramatically.

"A pair of tiny black eyes peered into the room and found little Mary. Attached to the eyes was the most hideous, twisted and wrinkled face Mary had ever seen. Her mouth opened into a tiny O as six more demented creatures appeared in the door."

"Oh no, Miss!" said Howard. "Are they going to eat her?"

Emmy smiled in reassurance. "The first creature's repulsive face broke into a perfectly friendly smile." Several of the children sighed in relief.

"Oh, how lovely," said Florence after hearing that the dwarves offered to pay Mary in gold for her work.

"She washed the bed clothes and set the room straight, being careful to dust all of the surfaces and furniture and to sweep under the rug," Emmy continued.

"It's not very spooky," interrupted Tommy with

a furrowed brow. "It's only about housekeeping."

Emmy narrowed her eyes at the boy and he ducked his head in shame. Emmy told of Mary's diligence until her month was nearly through.

"'I've been working so hard all this month,' she yawned. 'A little nap won't hurt.'

"She lay on top of her bed without even making it and drifted off to sleep for much longer than she planned. When she woke, the sun was already high in the sky and she had to hurry to catch up with the cooking and cleaning.

"'I won't sweep under the rug today,' she said. 'I just did it yesterday and no one looks there anyway.'

"She hurried through her chores and had the meat and bread ready just in time for supper. The dwarves thanked her and shook her hand for her good work that month, but they seemed to be looking at her with suspicion and there was no talk of the gold they would give her.

"Mary felt troubled as she set her head on her pillow that night. 'I feel like I've forgotten something,' she muttered, but she blew out her lamp and settled in to sleep.

"Almost immediately, Mary was dreaming. Insects were crawling through her window and oozing down her wall. They were making a dreadful, high-pitched noise and Mary covered her hands with her ears."

"Oh, it's dreadful, Miss," said Cassie, covering her eyes with both hands.

"Then the windows began to rattle until a gust of wind blew them open. Mary cowered in her nightgown on her bed against the wall. She tried to pull her quilt around her, but the wind kept pulling it off. Owls were hooting. In the distance, she heard a wolf howl."

"Is it almost over?" said Tilly, clasping her hands together. None of the boys squirmed or complained now. Emmy nodded and continued.

"The insects kept up their noise and Mary began to decipher their words.

"'Dust under the rug. Dust under the rug.'

"Mary tried to cover her ears, but the chant would not cease. Then suddenly the wind stopped, the shutters closed, and all of the crawly creatures disappeared. Mary woke up in a sweat and sat up in her bed.

"She put on her slippers, pulled on her shawl and rushed to find the broom in the closet. 'I was wrong to leave it,' she told herself. 'Even if no one else knows, I will.' She grabbed the broom from against the wall and began to sweep the dust out from under the dwarves' large woollen rug. When she had finished, there appeared before her a chest full of gold and jewels. The little men tumbled out of their beds and circled around Mary who stared at the chest in wonder.

"'You've passed the test and broken the spell,' they cheered.

"'What do you mean?' said Mary.

"The oldest dwarf took her hand and led her to her chair. 'We wanted to give you your fair reward, but only someone honest and true could earn this treasure. By sweeping under the rug when no one else would know, you proved yourself, Miss Mary.'

"Mary began to cry with relief. 'I nearly left it, Jacques. I thought no one would know, but my conscience wouldn't allow it.'

"Jacques patted her hand and passed her a cup of tea. 'Where would any of us be without our conscience?' he said. 'But you're special for having listened to yours and now your family will be provided for as long as you live.'

"Mary tidied up after breakfast and then bid her friends goodbye. On top of her reward she had learned a most valuable lesson. She couldn't wait to share it with her little family."

Some of the children let out a sigh of relief and little siblings hugged their older brother's or sister's, but Emmy overheard Sam whisper to Arthur "It was just a trick to get us to mind our P's and Q's. Dust under the rug. Really."

Emmy smiled and pretended she hadn't heard.


The following morning, after reading aloud several poems about autumn, Emmy had the students write a frightening composition. She wrote the phrase "The wind howled eerily through the barn. . ." to get the students started. She noticed several of them rewrote her story about the dust under the rug. She knew this was an excellent way to get into writing and praised little Cassie and Howard for their additions to the tale.

"A ghost at the window would certainly frighten me," she said to Howard, ignoring the dirt behind his ears. She'd forgotten to do the morning hygiene inspection in her excitement to begin her lessons.

But she was most surprised by Sam's writing. Sam was always reluctant to write anything. He needed a lot of encouragement to start and then took longer than everyone else to write even a sentence, but today he was inspired.

"The wind howled eerily through the barn the night Ol' Winslow disappeared. He told his wife he'd gone down to the barn to tend the cow, but he never returned.

"She waited until midnight before she went to look for him. He sometimes came in late when he got to sitting and remembering his life in the Old Country, but never this late. The wind whipped her skirt about her legs as she held her lamp out before her. Then it blew out the light and she had to trust her memory to find the dilapidated building.

"She heard the wind through the barn before she came to it. It sounded like a screaming banshee and she froze in terror of what might be inside."

"You've used wonderful vocabulary," Emmy said. Sam nodded his head and hesitated over the page. She moved away, fearing she had made him self-conscious. As the oldest student in the class, Emmy knew Sam preferred not to be held up as an example to others. With his quiet dedication and steady work ethic, it was tempting to point him out to the other students, but doing so seemed to make him shrink, so Emmy tried to let his work speak for itself.

The children worked diligently on their compositions much longer than they normally did. She chose several to share their writing with the class after recess by the fire. It was an enjoyable way to spend a fall afternoon. She could think of nowhere else she'd rather be. Her class of children from many backgrounds and distances were becoming her own.

The next morning, she woke with a throbbing head. Her neck ached and she felt her stomach quivering. She hurried to the outhouse just in time and then returned to do her best to prepare for a day of teaching with the flu. She forced down a piece of toast and a fortifying cup of tea and then trudged the distance to school. Snow flurries swept around her, but she focused on being grateful for the cool air on her hot temples.

Her legs were trembling by the time she arrived, and she put a kettle on to the stove as soon as she got it going. Fortunately, her mother had sent a packet of tea in her last care package. Emmy looked over her plans and made adjustments to allow herself time to sit. She copied as much work as she could on to the blackboard and then placed her head on her arms for a few minutes before the children arrived.

"You look like death." Bev frowned.

Emmy pressed her lips into a smile. "I'll be alright," she said.

Bev's brows met in consternation and Emmy felt a tiny bit better that someone cared. Then Mrs.

Drummond arrived with a package filled with scribblers.

"Emmy's not well," Bev said, wringing her hands.

"I'll be fine," Emmy said, pushing herself to stand.

Mrs. Drummond tested Emmy's temperature with the back of her hand and shook her head. "I'd stay if I could, but my husband needs me to help mend the fence today. I'll tell my Florence to do as much as she can. She's a good girl."

"Yes, thank you," Emmy said. Then her ears began to ring. She felt like she was in a tunnel of pain and fever.

Mrs. Drummond dug into her purse. "Here, I'll leave these with you. They're Aspirin. Don't worry about returning them. If there are any left, I'll collect them the next time I'm in." She patted Emmy's shoulder and left with a few concerned glances at Emmy on her way out.

Emmy swallowed one of the pills and lifted the bell to ring the children inside.

Somehow, she made it through the next three days of fever and nausea by calling on the older students more frequently to teach the younger students. The classroom was noisier than usual, but Emmy didn't have her usual energy to keep a tight reign. She was grateful it was the end of October and not September. Their routine was firmly established, and she could blame the extra noise on excitement over writing Halloween poems and making Halloween crafts. Patsy brought in a pumpkin to be carved the first day of Emmy's illness which started the other families on donating their pumpkins to the cause. They counted pumpkin seeds and roasted them on the stove, carved elaborate faces and told all sorts of pumpkin stories. But she was relieved when the weekend came and allowed herself the first lie-in she'd had since boarding at the Blaine's house.

Emmy woke to a pounding on her door. "Yes?" her voice was weak.

"Dad says it's time to get up," said a young voice she couldn't distinguish through the fog of her illness and exhaustion.

Emmy groaned, but forced her aching body out of bed and into her clothes. She squinted at her watch which read half past eight and groaned again. Why were they waking her? She wasn't their child.

She stepped into the hall and nearly bumped into Cassie.

"Good morning," she said to the scared little girl. She was hiding something behind her back.

"I saved this, Miss," Cassie said and looked about. Then, she held out half a piece of toast. "Dad said he doesn't allow laziness in his house and that you aren't to have any breakfast, but I noticed you weren't feeling well this week."

Emmy felt a rush of indignation. How dare he? The juxtaposition of his daughter's empathy only made it worse. She swallowed the words that were fighting to spew out of her mouth to crouch down and smile at her student. "Thank you," she whispered, taking the soggy piece of toast out of Cassie's tight grip and slipping it into her apron. "That was very thoughtful." She tapped the girl on her nose to bring out a smile and then returned to her room for her purse and coat.

"I'm going to Mrs. Drummond's," she said to Mrs. Blaine.

Mrs. Blaine looked pale and frightened, not unlike her daughter. "I'm so sorry miss. He said you weren't to have any breakfast. He don't believe in sleeping in." But she pushed a concealed cloth filled with raisins into Emmy's hand. Emmy wanted to refuse the food, not wanting to have any part in Mr. Blaine's bullying or the secrets they kept to avoid him. But she knew raisins were dear and saw concern in Millie's pale blue eyes.

Emmy placed the raisins in her pocket next to the squished toast. "Thank you. I'll be back before sundown." She didn't ask if she'd be allowed to take supper with them. She'd rather starve.

Dry snowflakes whipped at her face as she hurried to Mrs. Drummond's farm. She hoped she wouldn't get lost. Mrs. Drummond had pointed out the way when they drove to town, but Emmy hadn't actually been there before. She hoped she would be welcomed. Even if she wasn't, staying outside in the frigid weather was better than staying in that house with that, that . . .man. If she had to, she could go to the school and light a fire and drink some tea. She pulled her coat more tightly around her trembling body. She wasn't sure if she was shaking with hunger, sickness or anger.

It took about an hour, but she arrived at a comfortable looking farm house and knocked at the door. "Miss Bennett!" Florence greeted her with a smile. "We weren't expecting you. Come in!" She ushered Emmy in while calling down the hall. "Mom, Miss Bennett's here!"

They had an open coatroom with plenty of hooks and boots lined up neatly. A pleasant parlour off the right and was decorated with floral wallpaper and doilies on every surface. Mary came to the door wearing an apron and wiping her hands on a towel. Her face was red and perspiring and her hair stood out in all directions. "Well! To what do we owe this great honour?" she finished wiping her hand and held it out. Emmy forced down her anger to smile and shake Mrs. Drummond's hand.

"Och, I see," Mrs. Drummond squinted her eyebrows. "Florence, take your brothers out to the barn to play. I need to talk to your teacher in private."

"But mother. . ." Florence said.

"I'll have none of your cheek, young lady. Do as you're told and if you're good, I'll let you in for tea with Miss Bennett after a spell."

Florence hurried out, tossing a pleading look behind her.

Mary peered more closely at Emmy. "At first, I

thought you were looking better with that colour in your cheeks, but I see now, it's no healthy glow. You're quite peaked," Mary led Emmy to a chair in the kitchen. She tried not to groan as she settled herself. The warmth was almost painful to her frozen toes and cheeks.

"Now, what has that man done?" Mary said.

Emmy looked about her, worried about little ears.

"Don't you worry," Mary said. "My children know when to be scarce."

Emmy began. "I slept in today. I've been so ill."

"And well you should have. The Blaines should have kept their children clear away to let you rest, but I think I can guess where this is going."

"Mr. Blaine told Cassie to knock on my door to wake me up at 8 to tell me I wouldn't be allowed any breakfast for sleeping in."

Mary stood up, gathering her kettle, a cup and saucer, plate, biscuits and jam. "For shame. He did that just to spite you."

Emmy wished she could lay her pounding head on the table or curl up on the sofa she could see through the kitchen door. Instead, she made herself smile. "Thank you for understanding."

Mary shook her head and continued preparing tea. "I wanted you to come live with us, but Mr. Blaine insisted. He hates having me on the board to begin with.

"We had a teacher once, you see. He blamed us for letting Mr. Withers fall in love and move to another town. Humph." She threw up her hands in annoyance. "Mr. Withers was in love when he came to us. Can't stop such a thing. And the other town offered him more money and older students. We couldn't compete."

She placed some heavily buttered toast in front of Emmy. Her mouth watered. "Don't wait for me, Miss Bennett. I've already had my breakfast. Tuck in."

Emmy placed a spoonful of the proffered marmalade onto the warm toast and ate while Mary continued.

"He's a hard man, Mr. Blaine. I've heard his father whipped him. I don't think he whips his children, but there's the old belief that spoiling a child is the worst sin. Do you know folk like that?"

Emmy nodded. She knew the philosophy intimately.

"Treats his wife the same, I believe. Takes the "Head of the house" a bit too literally. Must be a daunting, taking everything on your own shoulders like that. Not letting yourself show weakness. Or love. . ." Mary paused and took a deep breath. "But you've allowed me to start gossiping. I need to hold my tongue. Harold is always saying so and I know he's right." She paused to pour tea.

"Thank you," Emmy said. "It's very good of you to serve me. I shouldn't have bothered you."

Mary stopped pouring tea and put her hands on her hips. "And who should you bother, if not me? We've taken you from your family, your mother. Someone's got to take care of you. I'd be offended if you'd turned to anyone else." She finished pouring Emmy's tea, placed a plate of biscuits between them and then sat to pour herself a cup.

"I'm very pleased you came, yes," Mary said. "No one to talk to most days but my squabbling children and grumpy husband," she chuckled. "Not that they get much better with their overbearing Mama and wife."

"Your children are very well behaved at school," Emmy said. "And they're coming along extremely well in their studies."

Mary patted her hand. "There, there. Glad to hear it. Have you had any news from home?"

Emmy shared her latest letter and talked about her younger brothers and sisters. Her headache lessened as she turned her mind to other things. She reached into her purse to return the Aspirin, but Mary wouldn't allow it. "You're still not over it, I can tell. Keep those. I have plenty more."

Mary invited the children to join them and they took turns telling her about their chickens, favourite games and cousins in the neighbouring farm. "They're too young for school this year, but Elaine will be joining us next fall," Florence said. "She's the prettiest little thing."

"Don't you go making her vain, my love," her mother said. "Although she does have the most beautiful blond curls."

Emmy had nearly forgotten the time when Mr. Drummond came into the kitchen looking for lunch. "I should be on my way," Emmy stood to leave.

"Oh dear, don't go on my account," Mr. Drummond's face was red and shiny. She instantly knew he was nothing like Mr. Blaine or her stepfather. His children ran to hug him, and he wrestled a moment with the boys and patted Florence's long plait with a look of admiration.

"Come help me get lunch on," Mary said. "We'll drive you home in time for supper."


Emmy felt considerably better after a day with the Drummonds. She learned that Mary had been a teacher herself before she was married.

"I see myself in you, Miss Bennett," Mary said while they set the table. "You don't take any foolery, but still you're gentle with the little 'uns. No use being cruel. Some teachers think that's what you have to do," she sniffed. "But I always found a firm and gentle hand was the best medicine. Never found any use for the strap. Sitting in the corner did well enough."

Emmy was relieved to hear it. Mr. Blaine frequently admonished her to use the strap liberally, especially as she was a woman, but she never responded to his opinion and wouldn't say whether she used the strap or not. She clearly remembered losing all respect for a teacher who lost his temper and strapped seven children in one day. He may have put fear into them for the day, but soon after, they went back to mocking the pimple-faced teacher behind his back.

The following day Emmy's flu lifted, but she discovered most of the household had developed her symptoms. She wished Mr. Blaine would get sick, but he continued as strong as a tank and demanded his family continue with their regular chores. Emmy helped Millie and the children whenever she could.

# CHAPTER ELEVEN

*Halloween*

Thursday was Halloween and Emmy heard the children talking excitedly on the playground.

"The radio said aliens were invading the earth!" lisped Betsy Hamm first thing in the morning. "We were all so afraid! We took turns listening to the headset. Papa didn't believe us when we started screaming and crying, so he took the headset and started to get a real fearful look in his eyes."

Betsy's sister Jane continued the story. "Then it turned out to be a big hoax! Mr. Welles was only acting and then Papa got real angry and sent us all to bed."

By then a knot of children surrounded the girls and as each one joined, the story needed retelling. Most families, the Blaine's included, could not afford a radio and so had missed the drama. The children, who were already excited by the fact that it was Halloween, became even more agitated and

Emmy rang the bell early.

As she took attendance and worked through the morning routine she formulated a plan. She glanced at the work she'd put on the board. They should finish that first. They would be motivated if they knew what was coming.

"Children, I am pleased to tell you I have a very special lesson planned today. Before we can get to it; however, we must complete the work on the blackboard. We need as much time as possible for our special lesson, so I'll check the work of the older classes and our oldest students will check the work of the younger students. I want to invite Miss Lafferty's class to join ours, so I will need you all to work very quietly so I can speak to her. You may begin."

That stopped the happy chatter and heads bent over slates to complete arithmetic and grammar. Emmy only had to give out a few reminders to work neatly for the whole class to get the message. She left her door open as she took a moment to share her idea with Bev. Her eyes sparkled as she agreed to the scheme and Emmy returned to her classroom.

The children were done their work and corrections in half an hour. Then, Patsy and Sam helped her wipe the boards clean and Emmy used her neatest script to write "The War of the Worlds" at the top of the first board. Whispers of interest broke out, but Emmy clapped her hands.

"Last night, some of you heard a most unusual radio broadcast," she said. Several hands waved for attention. Emmy patted them down with a single motion. "Unfortunately, I, like many of you, missed the story and would like to hear all about it. I heard the broadcast when it first came out in 1938, and some people really believed aliens were landing! It is such a good play, I would like our class to work with Miss Lafferty's to rewrite and recreate The War of the World."

Murmurs rumbled through the little room and several students wriggled in their seats. Bev poked her head into the classroom and Emmy beckoned her class to join them.

"We have a lot to do to complete this in one day." She took up her chalk and made a list. "We need to write the script first, of course. Those who heard the broadcast will be our experts. I will take dictations on the blackboard while some of you copy the words to be used for practicing our own radio play. We will also need costumes and sound effects," she added to her list. "Fortunately, some of you are already in costume for Halloween, but we all need a costume. We'll have to make do with what we can find at the school. Finally, we will need actors and an audience. Consider which you would prefer."

She allowed the students a moment to chat about the thrilling day plan. She was feeling rather eager herself and it didn't take much to rein in the energy and begin writing out the play. Emmy and Bev gathered the children at the front of the classroom while Patsy, Jane and Betsy took turns telling the story. They had each heard different parts, since only two people could listen to the radio headset at once. They occasionally disagreed on story points, but Emmy reminded them they were making the story their own and so it didn't necessarily need to be exact. The other pupils listened with rapt attention until it drew near to recess. Then the little ones began to squirm, and Emmy released them to run and play while Bev kept an eye on the playground. Then they reconvened and found they had finished the script by 11:00. The five oldest students copied as she wrote on the board. They had six copies to use, including the one on the blackboard, to practice the play.

"Miss Bennett," Sam said to her at lunch time. "I'm not really fond of school. Most of the time, I'd rather be working at home with my Dad, but today is swell." His eyes shone, and Emmy felt it might have been worth living at the Blaine's house just to see Sam so enthusiastic.

"I'm so pleased," Emmy said. "You're doing excellent work. I can't wait to watch the result."

Emmy allowed Sam, who was playing the radio announcer, to take over as director after lunch while she worked with the shyer students who preferred to develop the props and costumes. She found a box of scrap material in the crawl space beneath the school as well as some needles and thread. Georgia, Betsy and Florence helped her sew an alien costume while Bev took the boys to the barn to look for scrap boards they could bang together. They also found broken desks and tables they were trying to transform into a crashed alien space craft.

Rosemond Purdy proved to be quite an excellent pianist. She played in the background between scenes, as happened in the radio broadcast.

They took a short break for lunch, but the children asked to skip their recess in order to get back to work on the production. By two o'clock, they deemed the play ready to perform. Emmy wished she had invited the parents to watch, but she had only planned the whole thing that morning. There was no point inviting the older classes who would only tease the little children and cause a ruckus. So, she and Bev were the audience members and Emmy allowed herself to sink into the horrifying imagined alien invasion on a dark and stormy Hallowe'en afternoon.

Sam's voice changed into the cadence of a radio announcer. If Emmy closed her eyes while Rosemond played she could almost imagine she was on an elegant stage in New York City. Tommy Blaine was a believable reporter in Princeton and Oscar Fleishman stumbled only occasionally in his part as Professor Pierson. It would be a truly frightening play if one believed it were true. Emmy had never read the War of the Worlds herself, but now that she'd seen her class throw themselves into acting out the story, she wondered if she could get a copy to read to the class through the long, cold winter.

When Sam read his final, hopeful monologue, Emmy felt her heart would nearly explode with pride. Suddenly there was a bang on the schoolroom door. Emmy's eyes flew open and she saw Mr. Blaine stalk into the school. He furrowed his forehead as he took in the scene before him. "Miss Bennett, I have come to collect my children early," he said. "There seems to be quite a storm brewing."

"Of course," said Emmy, though she wondered how he meant her to return home.

"What exactly are you are teaching them?" he said as she stood to gather his children. Emmy saw Bev stiffen with fright.

Sam ran up to his father, beaming. "Dad, we've been acting," he said, eyes glowing. "I had the main part and I was director."

"You've been acting in a play?" said Mr. Blaine as though sniffing a soiled diaper. "Shakespeare or something?"

"No Dad," Sam's smile faltered. "Something modern, performed only last night on the radio station."

Tommy had run up to fill in the rest. "We've spent the whole day preparing. Perhaps you could stay to watch it again."

Mr. Blaine glared at Emmy. "The entire day, Miss Bennett? I thought we'd discussed the importance of covering the curriculum quickly throughout the year."

Emmy felt like spitting in his eye, but she clenched her fists to remain calm. "I can assure you this fits entirely into the curriculum and, in fact, goes quite beyond. The children were writing and reading all day. Arithmetic was required in measurements for costumes and sets and the students were learning some geography as part of the play."

Mr. Blaine narrowed his eyes. "None of this

comes from the readers or study books you've been given. I expect you to catch up the children tomorrow on everything they've missed in today's. . . foolery. I don't know what you're used to, but we only do plays for Christmas and Spring Concerts around these parts.

"Alistair, Katherine, William and Cassie, collect your things. I want to be going immediately."

Emmy stood aside and said nothing as the Blaine children obeyed their father. When they left the room, all the liveliness of their special day left with them and Emmy was left shaking with anger to try to put her classroom back in order with the disappointed children that remained. Mr. Blaine's cutting words left them all with a covering of shame. "Oh dear," Bev murmured.

# CHAPTER TWELVE

*Frostbite*

November was born on a frightful snowstorm. Even so, Emmy dressed for school in a dress and stockings, like any other day. She left early, before the children were ready. She couldn't wait to be away from Mr. Blaine and his stony silence since the day before.

The snow was past her ankles when she left the farm house and kept falling into her boots. She was a quarter of the way to school when Mr. Blaine passed her in his horse and buggy, spraying her with snow. She knew he had an appointment that morning in the next town. She pressed her mittened hands together, trying to erase her anger as well as warm herself. Five minutes later, she came upon him again, stuck in the snowy ditch.

"Miss Bennett, I need your help," he said, his voice brusque.

"I don't know how to fix your buggy, sir," she

said and attempted to move on without stopping, as he had.

He grabbed her arm and she cried out in alarm.

"Move to the back and push when I say so." He gestured with his thumb.

Emmy pulled her arm away the moment he loosened his grip. "I'm not your property to be ruled over," she said.

Mr. Blaine whipped his head around. "I'll not be spoken to in that way, girl. You live under my roof, you'll obey my orders."

"And what if I don't?" Emmy crossed her arms and stared at the man.

"I wouldn't recommend that." His voice was low and Emmy felt more frightened of him than she ever had been in her life. She held her ground a moment, but then considered what it would be like to live in the same house afterward. She stomped toward the back of the buggy and pushed. Mr. Blaine returned to the driver's seat and held on to the reins.

"Push!" he shouted and smacked the horse with the reins as she leaned into the buggy. The wheels sprayed mud and ice onto her stockinged legs and the bottom of her dress. "Push!" he shouted again, and she placed all her anger into shoving. "Push!" he said again and again. Emmy's arms shook with the effort and her legs grew colder and colder.

"Dammit, push harder, useless girl," he spat. She stopped pushing and kicked the buggy with her boot just in time to watch the wheels swerve and slide back onto the road. Emmy slipped and fell onto the icy snow and looked up to see Mr. Blaine slap his reins and speed away. She was furious, but there was nothing to do but haul herself up and hurry on to school. She saw her stockings were cut and her leg was bleeding, but she couldn't feel anything, and she wasn't going to be late on account of Mr. Blaine. She pulled her coat around her body and leaned her head into the wind and snow.

When she arrived at the schoolhouse, it was nearly as cold inside as it was out, but her anger and humiliation over the incident with Mr. Blaine fuelled her and she had the fire going sooner than any other morning. While she stood before the inefficient stove, her legs throbbed in pain. She took some time to survey the damage and saw that, on top of her ripped stockings and her bleeding legs, she had frostbite. Her legs stung as they warmed, and took on a blue, mottled look. "Blast that man!" she hollered into the empty building.

November remained frigid and Emmy had only one pair of decent stockings left. She still hadn't received any payment for teaching. She planned to bring this issue up first thing at the next school board meeting. She took to wearing a pair of torn stockings underneath her final good pair. Her legs continued to be sensitive to the cold when she walked to and from school and she wanted to avoid more frostbite. Blisters rose where the skin had frozen and those areas felt naked in the freezing wind. She cursed Mr. Blaine silently every time she felt them burn.

Anne and Mel's classes continued to disintegrate and sometimes she overhead them saying "Emmy and Bev have such easy classes. If only they knew how hard we work." It made Emmy's blood boil, knowing very well that consistent discipline and effort would solve their problems. She hoped for changes in the upcoming school board meeting.

The opportunity came on the last Friday of the month. She and Bev whispered together as they prepared for school that morning.

"Is there anything we can say about the upper grades?" Bev said as she struggled to pin her hair before a cloudy mirror.

"I don't see how. We need to bide our time. I'm sure the children have told their parents what's happening in their classrooms." Emmy tried to hide the run in her stockings.

Bev let out an exasperated puff of air and slammed her comb onto her desk. "I just can't abide how our school sounds like a circus."

"Let me help." Emmy reached out to smooth her friend's hair.

Bev smiled. "Thanks Emmy. I always get so worked up on school board days. I worry they'll find some fault."

Emmy popped a pin into place. Bev's hair was back in control. "You have nothing to worry about. You're a wonderful teacher."

Bev patted her hair and turned to hug her friend. "I'm so glad you came here with me. I can't imagine teaching alone with Mel and Anne."

Bev and Emmy heard a knock and were surprised to find Mr. Blaine, Mr. Purdy and Mr. Fell waiting on the school steps.

"Good morning," Emmy said. "I'm sorry if we've kept you waiting."

"Not at all," Mr. Harding smiled, but there was something stern in his eyes. "It's come to our attention that we haven't visited the school yet this year. We'd like to have a better understanding for our meeting tonight."

"Of course," said Bev.

"Try to pretend we aren't here," Mr. Fell said. "We'd like to see things as they are."

Emmy doubted she could do such a thing, but she needed to prepare. She and Bev parted ways in the hall with a raised eyebrow. How would Anne and Mel behave around the school board members?

Emmy reviewed her day plan and made a few adjustments, sharpened pencils and checked for clean slates and orderly school books. She considered cancelling the little play the children would be doing before recess, but they would be so disappointed, she left it. She copied her lessons onto the board.

Out the window, she noticed the board members checking the facility and making note of a few maintenance issues. Mr. Purdy hammered some nails back in place along the fence. She also heard them in the hallway and staff room and then Mr. Fell popped his head into Emmy's classroom.

"Good morning Miss Bennett. Everything looks ship shape. Do you happen to know when Miss Miller and Miss Fleming will arrive?"

Emmy lowered her hand to face Mr. Fell. Should she tell him the truth? "They should be along shortly," she said.

Mr. Fell nodded and stepped further into her room. "Do you mind if I look at your day plan?"

"Not at all," she said, glad she had taken some extra time to ensure it was complete.

Anne and Mel arrived when the bell rang. Emmy spotted them with their heads close together, lost in conversation. She did not tell them the school board members were waiting in their classrooms. She eyed Bev across the hall and shook her head slightly.

"Good morning," Bev said, but Anne and Mel ignored her.

Emmy continued with her morning as usual, although she frequently wondered what was happening in Mel and Anne's classes. Just before 10:00, Mr. Fell appeared in her doorway.

"Good morning," she said, mid-reading lesson. The children sat at attention and turned their heads, almost as one, to see their visitor.

"Class, Mr. Fell is visiting to see what we are learning."

The children greeted Mr. Fell and a smile replaced his initial look of wild concern. "Good morning children. Please carry on."

"Hi Daddy!" squeaked his son, George.

Mr. Fell nodded and moved to the back of the classroom.

Emmy and her class continued preparing their play. A few days ago, she had read them a story from their reader called The Snow Blanket about the coming of winter. After reading it again, she had the children rewrite the story into speaking parts. She had the oldest students copy out the little play for each of the readers. The youngest children were the seeds and snow and only said a few lines in chorus. The older children were the North wind, Mother Earth, the Frost King, Cloud, Sun and Ocean. They had made little masks out of paper to show which character was which.

"We are very fortunate to have Mr. Fell as our audience today. It is only a rehearsal, Mr. Fell, but we hope you will enjoy our efforts." When she was done explaining and the children set to work, Mr. Fell stood beside her.

"I've never seen reading taught in such a way. Is this something you learned at Teacher's College?"

"No, sir," Emmy smiled. "My school teacher did something similar when I was a girl. I've had to adapt a bit to the younger classroom, but they have enjoyed the added responsibility. I find it helps them understand the story more deeply."

Mr. Fell chuckled. "George is certainly enjoying his role as the Frost King. I've never heard him read so well." Mr. Fell rocked on his heels and stood tall.

Emmy agreed. "He's a bright boy."

Mr. Fell ambled through the classroom and even tried on George's Frost King mask and read a line. Then he nodded farewell and Emmy took a deep breath of relief.

"Thanks a lot," Anne hissed in Emmy's ear while she watched the children from the school steps at recess.

"How was your morning?" Emmy did not look at her colleague.

"Why didn't you warn us they were coming?"

Emmy turned to look at her accuser. "We had no time. You were late for school."

Anne rolled her eyes and stretched herself to full height. "We were not late, Emmy Bennett. Don't come at me with that holier-than-thou attitude. Those of us with more experience don't need to waste so much time pouring over lesson plans."

Emmy turned her eyes and her body away from Anne. "Then I have no idea why you're angry at me." She marched down the stairs toward the children and, more importantly, away from Anne.

The school board members assembled in front of the school before the end of the day. They were supposed to meet at 4:00, giving the teachers an hour to properly tidy and prepare the school house. Emmy made sure her students did as much of the cleaning as possible before they were dismissed.

"We're having special guests at the school house tonight. We want our classroom to look its very best."

The children seemed pleased to help and some of the girls offered to cut out snowflakes to brighten the classroom. Emmy allowed Shirley, who was the best at drawing, to decorate the blackboard with a winter scene. She thanked her class for their keen effort as they filed out the door.

Anne and Mel supervised their classes as they left the building. Mel's eyes were wide and her hair disheveled. Anne looked furious.

As soon as the students cleared out, Mr. Blaine, Mr. Fell, Mr. Purdy and Mrs. Drummond entered the school house.

"Good afternoon," Mr. Fell greeted them. "I'm sorry to surprise you with this early visit, but we feel it is necessary." He paused to look each of them in the eye. Emmy returned his gaze without flinching.

"We have some serious concerns. We must deal with them immediately."

Mel's eyes seemed to be jumping all over the place. From Mr. Fell to Mr. Blaine to Mr. Purdy to Anne, then down to the floor and up to the ceiling, like a bouncy ball. Anne stared straight ahead with a stony expression. Her jaw seemed tight enough to break. Bev wrung her hands.

"We'd like to meet with you individually," said Mr. Fell. "Please remain in your classrooms until we've spoken to you. We want to begin with you, Miss Miller."

For the first time, Anne's rigid shoulders sagged, but she nodded her acceptance and followed the men to her classroom.

"I'm so afraid," Mel's screechy voice echoed in the hallway before she spun on her heel and scurried to her classroom.

"You have nothing to worry about," Emmy reassured Bev. "This is not about us."

"I feel badly for Mel and Anne," said Bev.

"Don't waste your worry on them," Emmy said and they turned to wait in their own classrooms.

Emmy cleaned the chalkboards, straightened desks and books and tried to plan for the following day. She was just selecting a class dictation when she looked up at the sound of a door opening. Heavy footsteps clumped down the hallway and out the door. Anne looked neither left nor right on her way out of the school.

"What do you think happened?" Bev whispered from her doorway.

"We can't know until they tell us." They turned to see the four school board members cross the hall into Mel's classroom before they returned to their desks.

Emmy's classroom was the last they visited. By then, Emmy had planned her entire week and the week after, though she wondered at the quality of the plan when her mind kept drifting elsewhere. She checked her pocket mirror again to make sure her hair was in place.

"Thank you for waiting, Miss Bennett," said Mr. Fell. "I'm sure it's been a rather long day."

"Not at all," she said. Only her chair was large enough to seat an adult, so they stood in a circle. "I'm sorry our desks are so small."

"Don't mind standing at all," Mr. Purdy smiled.

"Miss Bennett, we wanted to tell you we are pleased with the work you've been doing here in Harding," Mr. Fell said.

Although Emmy had been certain of her good work, she couldn't help smiling at the reassurance. "Thank you, sir."

"You came with a good reference and you don't disappoint," Mrs. Drummond said.

"I was most intrigued by your lesson in reading," said Mr. Fell who seemed to be searching the class-room for more masks.

"I was following my teacher's example."

"Yes. We appreciate teachers who can accept suggestions," Mrs. Drummond said and cleared her throat. Emmy took advantage of the pause.

"Mr. Fell, Mr. Purdy, Mr. Blaine and Mrs. Drum-mond, thank you for these kind words. I hope you don't mind if I ask a question."

The board looked at one another in surprise. "Of course," said Mr. Fell.

"It was my understanding, when I was hired, that all teachers would receive the same wages in this school."

The three men looked at their shoes like chas-tened school boys while Mrs. Drummond's eyes sparkled encouragement. "Miss Miller and Miss Fleming told me they are receiving a considerably higher wage. Is that correct?"

Mr. Fell pursed his lips, but then looked her in the eye. "I'm afraid that's true. It has obviously been a mistake."

"I quite agree," Emmy waited until all three men returned her gaze. "I believe you have noticed that it has created a . . . division in our school. May I request we all receive the same remuneration, as previously promised?"

The men furrowed their brows and exchanged questioning looks. Mrs. Drummond pursed her lips.

"I don't need an answer immediately. You can get back to me," Emmy said.

Mr. Fell spoke first. "May we use your classroom for a few minutes?"

"Of course," Emmy replied. She hadn't expected such a quick response. She nodded at the board members and strode out of the classroom, pulling the door closed behind her.

Bev was waiting in her classroom with her coat and hat. "Aren't you finished yet?" she asked.

"I've asked about our wages."

Bev gasped. "Really? After this upsetting day. Where did you find the nerve?"

"They've seen for themselves what's happening here. It seemed like the right time."

"You're much braver than I." Bev shook her head.

"Did they give you a good report?"

Bev smiled. "Yes, thank you. Very good."

Emmy hugged her friend. "I knew they would. You're an excellent teacher."

"I feel like I still have so much to learn," Bev said.

"That's exactly how a good teacher should feel," said Emmy. She looked about Bev's tidy, happy classroom. "You don't have to wait for me, if you'd like to go home."

"Yes I do! I'm not going home without knowing how you are."

Emmy chuckled. "We'll walk together, then."

Emmy looked over some of Bev's students' work. "Dory's writing is really coming along," she said after reading her beautifully penned poem.

"Miss Bennett?" Mr. Fell poked his head into Bev's classroom.

"Yes?" asked Emmy.

"We're ready to see you. Thank you for waiting."

Emmy followed him back to the classroom. "Miss Bennett, you have brought up an important point," said Mr. Blaine, his arms crossed over his solid frame.

Emmy nodded, suddenly worried she had pushed too far.

"We'd like to make you a proposition," Mr. Fell continued. "Miss Miller has handed in her resignation this afternoon."

Emmy checked her expression. She did not want to appear shocked.

"She has a difficult class," Mr. Blaine continued. "We offered her extra pay in order to take these students. They're quite a challenge."

Emmy did not say that all children could be taught to mind their teachers.

"If you're willing to take her class, we'll happily adjust your income. Do you need some time to consider?" Mrs. Drummond finished their thought.

"When will Miss Miller's resignation come into effect?" Emmy asked.

"Immediately," Mr. Fell replied. "We need to hire a new teacher straight away. Fortunately, I have a niece nearby who is qualified to teach. However, I don't know that she could handle the middle upper class."

Emmy nodded, understanding the situation. "I accept your offer."

The three men exchanged looks of surprise. Mrs. Drummond only smiled "Th-that is very good of you. Thank you, Miss Bennett," said Mr. Purdy.

Emmy shook their hands and felt their overwhelming sense of relief.

"Emmy, are you absolutely sure?" Bev asked after Emmy explained the situation as they walked home.

"I expect it will be a lot of work at the start, but within a month, I believe they'll settle."

"I hope you're right," Bev shivered. "I wouldn't take them on if my wage were doubled."

Emmy smoothed her hair. "I'm sorry I didn't bargain for your wage to be increased," she said as the thought struck her. "We should all be paid the same."

"Oh no," Bev shook her head. "You deserve a raise for that class. Don't you worry about me."

Emmy tucked her hand into Bev's elbow. They walked on in a contemplative silence.

Their peaceful companionship was broken by the scene at the teacherage where Anne and Mel lived. They could hear yelling and breaking dishes as they passed.

"Should we just keep walking?" Bev whispered.

"I should find out what Anne has taught so far," Emmy asked. She strode up to the house and knocked, but the door was already partly open and swung open at her touch. The house was topsy turvy with Anne's packing and ranting.

"They think they know how to teach," Anne roared when Emmy and Bev entered. Three half-filled suitcases were sprawled about the parlour. Stockings and brassieres poked out of the cases in an unladylike fashion. Mel was perched on the arm of the sofa, wringing her hands. Both women stared at Bev and Emmy.

"We should go," Bev murmured.

"I'll make some tea," Emmy said and they hurried to the relative safety of the kitchen, but they could overhear.

"What will you do?" Mel said in her high-pitched, wavering voice.

"My Bart will be thrilled. We can get married next week." Anne clumped back and forth between her bedroom and the parlour.

"But you can't get married tomorrow. Where will you stay in the meantime?"

Anne's pacing stopped. "They'll have to give me my wages before I go. I'll stay in a hotel if I have to."

"Oh no," wailed Mel. "Go to my parents' house. I'll write a letter for you."

Emmy stole a peek into the living room as she set the table for tea. Anne was slumped on the sofa and Mel was scurrying about to find paper.

"That's good of you," Anne said. It was the kindest thing Emmy had ever heard her say.

"Emmy, I really think we should go," Bev was washing the stack of dirty dishes.

"We won't stay long" Emmy said.

"Tea's ready," Emmy called a few minutes later. She had found a tin of tea and a few biscuits in the messy kitchen and set out two chairs. She and Bev remained standing.

Only Mel came to the kitchen. "Anne really doesn't want you two here," she said. "We'll be fine on our own." But then her eyes widened in surprise at the tidy kitchen.

"I just want to find out what Anne covered this year," Emmy said.

"Why?" Mel's eyes narrowed.

"I'm going to be taking her class," Emmy smoothed out the dirty tablecloth, realizing this would only make Anne angrier.

Mel's mouth dropped open. "She's not going to like that. One. Bit."

Bev poured a cup of tea and handed it to Mel.

"We'll be leaving now. Perhaps you could have Anne write out a brief summary without telling her who it's for."

Mell took the proffered cup of tea and left the kitchen.

"Perhaps this wasn't such a good idea," Emmy said, reaching for her coat.

"Hmm, where have I heard that before?" Bev said. The two women left the house in a hurry.

# CHAPTER THIRTEEN

*Upper Graves*

Emmy experienced a difficult night. It took an age to fall asleep and then she kept waking every hour or so, worried about her new class. She would spend the weekend preparing the classroom. Not only would she need to plan Anne's lessons, she would have to undo the damage of at least a month of neglect, if not years beforehand.

Emmy rose just as light was beginning to stain the sky in pink and orange. Fortunately, the Blaines remained sleeping as Emmy prepared. She made a quick cup of tea and toast, left a note for Mrs. Blaine and stole out the door to scurry to the school house.

She drew in deep breaths of early morning air and tried to fill her head with the quietness. Emmy thought she was prepared for Anne's classroom, but it was even worse than she remembered. There was the dirty floor, the misaligned desks, the broken chalk and the smudged windows, but closer inspection revealed the damage and disrespect went further. Readers were ripped and littered with graffiti. Slates were broken, paper airplanes tossed about the classroom and spitballs stuck to the roof. She felt a glimmer of pity for Anne's inability to control these children, but it was soon replaced by anger over her incompetency and the effort it would take for Emmy to create order.

She ignored the student mess and focused on her new space. Anne's desk contained an apple core, cigarette ash (did she smoke in the classroom?), a tattered magazine and a drawer filled with unsharpened pencils. It would be easier to start with nothing.

Emmy threw away the core, ash, and magazine and wiped the desk until all the dust, sticky spots and smudges were gone. She sharpened the pencils and searched through the drawers for the register. It was tucked into the bottom drawer beneath a pile of ripped readers. Only the first day had been filled in. Even the simplest task had proven too difficult for Anne. Emmy placed the register on the desk and read over the names. It didn't seem to be complete.

Next, she searched for a lesson planning book, but as she suspected, she found nothing. She marched to her previous classroom to gather her small selection of personal items, including an empty scribbler. She returned to Anne's old classroom, laid the books in the teacher's drawer and opened the scribbler to the first blank page.

*November 13, 1939*

1. *Review register, create class seating arrangement.*
2. *Assign cleaning jobs: 3 stu•ents to sweep floor, 3 stu•ents to ti•y books, 3 stu•ents to clean ceiling, 3 stu•ents to •ust, 3 stu•ents to wash •esks, 3 stu•ents to supervise an• report to me, 3 stu•ents to erase pencil markings in rea•ers, 3 stu•ents to clean chalkboar•s an• copy out •ays lesson, 3 stu•ents to •raw water an• clean biffy. 27 stu•ents.*
3. *Discuss classroom expectations*
4. *Writing sample: Goo• citizenship in the classroom*
5. *Silent rea•ing while I assess*
6. *Recess, keep stu•ents in as necessary*
7. *Geography: Review of Cana•a. Move on to North America if time.*
8. *Lunch: Assign 2 playgroun• supervisors*
9. *Arithmetic: Review A••ition, Subtraction, Multiplication an• Division Tables*
10. *Spelling: Assign wor•s for the week. Compose sentences for each wor•.*
11. *Rea•ing •ictation.*
12. *Gym: Outsi•e soccer if stu•ents behave.*

She nodded her head at her lesson outline and then reviewed the Public School Curriculum and Teacher's Guide for grades seven and eight. The plan and review helped loosen the panic she'd been holding in her chest since she'd been asked to take the class. If she did all she could to be prepared, she would be ready for whatever they threw her way.

When Emmy had finished at the school, she decided to try the teacherage one more time. She found Anne gone and Mel moping on the sofa. Emmy removed her hat and sat opposite of Mel in the parlour.

"Mel, I'd like to ask if we could work together now that we're both in the upper grades."

Mel's distant gaze focused on Emmy. "You want to do work on the weekend?" she said.

"You've had the nines and tens for a month and I thought perhaps we could do a bit of planning and organizing."

Mel returned to staring out the window. "They have very different curriculum."

"Of course," Emmy said, doing her best not to let her irritation seep into her voice. "However, a joint effort on respect and courtesy in the school may be fruitful. I was thinking we could assign jobs to responsible students in the upper grades. Things like playground supervision and lunch supervision would be useful to all the teachers. Those who finish their work early could assist in Bev and Miss Fell's classrooms. I think it would help them feel more pride in their schooling experience, don't you?"

Emmy waited as Mel's face first wrinkled in thought and then cleared into a smile. "I remember when my teacher Miss Davidson used to have me help the little ones with their spelling. I'm a jolly good speller and the little ones loved to have a big girl work with them. That is an idea."

"I had a similar experience at my school," Emmy said. "There could be ribbons for best girl and boy at the end of the term or year. A little something to work toward."

Mel's head puckered again. "I don't know why Anne and I never thought of that. But it's really the boys that are the problem. I can't see them being inspired by supervising and helping."

Emmy shuffled an inch closer to her colleague. "I'm so pleased to have your input. I hardly know their names and you already know them."

"Well, I don't know about that," Mel said with a crooked smile. "I know Andy's fond of animals."

"The big boys in Shelby used to be in charge of the barn and horses," Emmy said as if she'd just thought of it.

"Yes. There's some would like that. And Mikey loves to lead sports."

"Excellent idea. He could lead a game at recess or even during physical education."

Mel relaxed and looked at Emmy in wonder. "I hope this works. I've been having an awful year. I can't imagine what it will be like without Anne to share my feelings."

Emmy chose her words carefully. "You two had a close friendship. I know I can't replace that, but I hope we can help one another."

Mel hesitated a moment and then held out her hand. "I'd like that," she said, and Emmy pressed her palm in agreement.

Monday morning arrived and so did Fanny Fell. She was fair and young with two blond braids running down her back. Emmy thought it would do her good to arrange her hair in a more grown up style, but she held her tongue.

"Pleased to meet you," Emmy said when Fanny entered the school.

Fanny's smile lasted only a moment and then jumped back into a worried line. "Hello. I hoped to come sooner, but my mother needed help with the canning this weekend. I'll be living with my Aunt and Uncle, not at the teacherage."

"I thought you might. Let me show you your classroom. I've started the stove. It's a little temperamental, so feel free to ask for help. There's a stack of wood for the day. I usually refill it every afternoon before I go home."

Fanny pulled out a notepad and began scribbling. Emmy paused her instructions until the girl stopped writing.

"Let me show you around the room." Emmy pointed out the maps, readers, drinking water and lunch box shelf. Then she showed her a seating chart and her plans for the week. Again, she waited for Fanny to record everything.

"You're welcome to change anything you like," Emmy said. "It's your classroom now, only I thought it would be helpful to have an idea of what they're used to. Children at this age do well with consistency."

Fanny nodded and scribbled.

"It's wonderful Miss Bennett. You've organized

everything so well. Thank you for being so kind."

Fanny's skin was frighteningly pale. Emmy patted her arm. "You'll do just fine. I often tell myself they're more afraid of me than I am of them. It's a lovely class."

Fanny's smile flittered and disappeared again. "I'm just kitty corner across the hallway." Emmy pointed. I'll introduce you to Bev before you settle in."

Bev was warm and welcoming and gave Fanny a cup of tea. As Bev asked the girl questions, Mel poked her head into the classroom. Bev and Emmy shared a look of surprise.

"Morning," her high-pitched voice bounced across the room. "I'm Mel. Thought I'd get an earlier start."

They exchanged introductions again and then Bev looked at her watch. "Sorry gals, I should get my ducks in a row. I hope you don't mind."

"Oh my," Fanny looked at her own watch. "How did it get so late already?"

Bev gave her a little hug. "Don't you worry. Take the morning to get to know them. Play a few games."

Emmy was feeling her own sense of anticipation. What if she was not able to control this unruly group? She shook away the thought and got to work.

As the children arrived, Emmy put on her coat and stopped by Bev's room. "We should invite Fanny, don't you think?" Bev said, already in her coat.

"I'll meet you outside." Emmy wanted to get an early start.

A light dusting of snow fell over the school yard but didn't deter the younger children from running around. "Good morning, Miss Bennett!" George Fell said as he whizzed past. Then, he stopped cold and plodded toward her with his head lowered. "My dad told me you won't be teachin' us anymore." He twisted his mouth to the side as if he were trying to keep from crying.

Emmy crouched down and placed a hand on his shoulder. Several other children from her primary class overheard and crowded around. Emmy waited for them to draw near and then stood to address them. "Boys and girls, I want to thank you for being such wonderful students this year. You might feel a bit sad to hear that I will start teaching the older grades now."

"But why?" wailed Shirley, her eyes round with shock.

"Miss Miller is needed elsewhere, and our school board asked me to take her class."

"Why can't they have someone else?" Jack interrupted. "You're our teacher."

Emmy looked at Jack with a stern eye. "Jack, please don't interrupt. All the children want a chance to hear what I have to say. Miss Fell will be your new teacher." She turned to invite Fanny to join them.

"Good morning," Miss Fell said to the gathered children.

"Miss Fell is a wonderful teacher and I know

you will treat her with kindness and respect. I will check in with her today to make sure you're all on your best behaviour."

"Miss Bennett has told me that you are very good students," Miss Fell said.

The children studied her, some wary, others curious.

"Now run along and play," Emmy said. "You haven't much time before the bell rings."

She nodded at Miss Fell, who seemed to be managing with the flock of girls who were questioning her. Emmy strode about the school yard, on the lookout for her new students.

She found a group of them standing in a circle behind the school. A thin whisper of smoke rose from the centre. "Good morning," Emmy said. A few jumped in alarm. Two even ran off.

"What do we have here?" she asked.

A tall boy with a pimply face sneered at her. "Why do you care? You ain't our teacher. Our teacher lets us do whatever we like."

"I will not have you speaking to me like this," Emmy said in a low voice. "In fact, I am your teacher. Miss Miller has resigned from Harding School."

The students had started a small grass fire between them.

"Timothy, will you kindly stomp out this fire," she said to one of the boys she knew by name.

"Yes, ma'am," the boy said, his head down.

"Maria, please draw a bucket of water to make sure this fire is properly snuffed." The older girl sneered and opened her mouth, but before she could complain, Emmy continued. "No objections. As far as I'm concerned, everyone around this circle, including the two who ran away took part in this fire. Off you go."

Maria heeded her instructions with a sigh and her friend Frances ran after to help.

"We'll discuss this further in class," Emmy promised, once the fire was out. She left the grumbling group and prepared to watch their behaviour in the hallway.

Her students tripped one another, hollered, ran and swore in the hallway. She said nothing but caught the eye of each offender and made a note in her book. The students exchanged questioning looks and whispered. Once all the students were inside, she closed the door and waited for them to take their seats. It took some time. She wanted to shout at them to sit and be quiet, but instead she waited, standing at the front of the classroom until most of the students eyed her warily.

"Good morning," she said. "I believe you know I'm Miss Bennett."

"Where's our real teacher?" said a brown-haired boy from the back of the classroom.

"I hear she got hitched," shouted Maria.

"That will be quite enough," Emmy's voice had a dangerous clip and the students grew quieter. "Miss Miller is no longer teaching here. I will be taking this class and Miss Fell will be teaching my former class.

"We have a lot of work ahead of us. I've seen the state of your classroom and your readers. I can only assume you're behind in your school work, so we have no time to waste." Timothy snickered from the left side of the classroom. Emmy gave him a stern look until he stopped.

"Please tell me your names, starting at the front of the classroom." She pointed at Timothy.

He cocked an eyebrow, stood and said, "I'm Mozart." Some of the students snickered and he took his seat with a smug expression. Emmy narrowed her eyes, said nothing, and looked to the next student.

"Robin Hood," said the next boy in line. The students tittered and whispered and continued with their charade. Apparently, Mary Scott, King George, Mary Contrary, Jack and Jill were all present in Emmy's classroom. Once she had gone through the entire classroom and only three students gave their real names, she wrote the three names on the board.

"Emily, Bertram and Sheila, thank you for your attention and respect. I would like to dismiss you fifteen minutes before lunch to have a short recess before you supervise the younger children. Is that acceptable?" The three students looked both surprised and pleased.

"Thank you, Miss," nodded Emily. Bertram and Sheila agreed.

"Who wants to watch those babies, anyway?" muttered Timothy.

"Timothy," Emmy wrote his name on the board. "For lighting a fire outside and swearing in the hallway, you will miss morning recess to sweep the floor." Timothy's eyes widened, but, for once, he said nothing. Emmy continued through her register list until she'd given each of the students who had misbehaved in the hallway or given her a false name a job to do at recess. The class was somewhat sobered when she finished.

"As you can see, there are consequences in my classroom for poor behaviour. I believe this is the best way to prepare you for life outside of school. As in real life, students who do their work and are respectful obtain certain rewards and privileges. I believe all of you are capable of receiving these rewards and privileges and I look forward to awarding these in the future.

"Miss Fleming and I have spoken and come up with several ideas for upper grade responsibilities. We will begin with lower grade supervision and hope to add other jobs as we see fit. I am also willing to hear your suggestions outside of teaching time."

Timothy raised his hand. "Miss, I don't like to watch the babies. I have to do that enough at home." He crossed his arms in front of him, challenging her.

"Perhaps you would prefer to referee a game of hockey," Emmy said. Timothy's eyes widened. "But first you'll have to show me you're capable of such a task."

"Now, I think we've spent enough time on classroom expectations. It's time to sing The Maple Leaf Forever and God Save the Queen."

Emmy was satisfied that her watchful eye and no-nonsense approach were having some effect. By recess, she was tired and wished she could escape for a cup of tea, but instead she kept the students in, as listed, to accomplish their tasks. There was grumbling, but after fifteen minutes, the classroom was beginning to look more acceptable. Timothy tried to shirk his sweeping duties by stopping to chat or tease, but Emmy kept on him until the worst of the dirt was swept away.

As she suspected, the reading and writing abilities of her class were extremely low. Obviously, it wasn't only Miss Miller who had not been able to control this class. They were far more than a month behind in their schoolwork. Emily stood out as the most capable, but even she had atrocious handwriting and large gaps in her knowledge of Canadian geography. Once Emmy had the class in hand, she would need to create a strict plan if she had any hopes of catching them up to grade level.

She kept only seven students in for half of lunch recess, but then she had a precious fifteen minutes to freshen up and eat her lunch.

"How are you managing?" Bev said as they passed in the staffroom.

"They'll learn, but it'll be a tough month."

Bev squeezed her shoulder and left to supervise the playground. Now that Miss Miller was gone, they had a supervision schedule. It wouldn't be just Bev and Emmy anymore. Mel slipped into the staffroom.

"I tried our responsibility rewards today," she said, unpacking her sandwich. "My class seems quite keen."

Emmy smiled, but she was too tired and hungry to talk. Mel didn't seem to mind and proceeded to share what seemed to be a minute-by-minute account of her morning. Emmy was pleased Mel was beginning to trust her, but she was happy to hear the bell, excusing her from the monologue.

"You leaving already?" Mel said. "I always wait until they've returned to class."

"I prefer to meet them in class. Gives me less to deal with at the start of the lesson."

Emmy left Mel pondering the idea.

Indeed, Emmy beat all of her students to class. Then, only two showed up. Emily and Sheila entered the class quietly and took their seats without meeting Emmy's eyes. Emmy greeted them and waited at the door for the others to appear. After five minutes, she said to the girls "Please read quietly until I return. Your classmates are late." Then, she marched to the playground, but it was empty. She continued to the back of the school, wary of fire or smoking, but she found no one.

She returned to the school and knocked on Bev's door. "Yes, Miss Bennett?" she asked.

"My class is missing," she said. "Did you happen to see where they went after lunch recess?"

Bev looked astonished. "No! I saw them milling together and I called them in, but then I left to look in at my own class. Oh, dear."

Emmy pressed her lips into a thin smile. "Not to worry. I'll get it sorted. Sorry to disturb you."

She returned to her classroom and found Emily and Sheila bent over their books. "Girls, it appears your classmates have decided they don't need to come to class. Do you happen to know where they went?"

Emily and Sheila looked at one another in fear. "I think they may have gone to Maria's house," said Sheila with a wavering voice. "Her parents are away."

"Thank you, Sheila. Weren't you girls tempted to join?"

"Oh no, Miss," Emily's eyes were earnest. "We hoped they wouldn't go. We thought it might be a joke. They wouldn't invite us."

Emmy stood with her hands on her hips for a moment while the girls exchanged nervous glances. "Well, there's no reason for you to miss out on your education due to the poor decisions of your classmates. Let's continue with arithmetic."

Emmy did her best to make the addition, subtraction, multiplication and division lesson fun. It was difficult when she was brimming with anger at the rest of her students, but she tried to keep herself from thinking of them too much. She was pleased to see Emily and Sheila showing a bit more of their personalities as she quizzed them and had them race one another to the answers.

"Well done girls. Since you were the only ones here to take part in the lesson, we have finished early. I think we'll take our gym class now and I'll let you choose what we do."

After a brief tête-a-tête, they chose skipping. Each girl had their own rope and Emmy joined them outside and turned the rope as they jumped and sang skipping songs.

"I'm sorry the other kids ditched your class," Emily said, breathless. "But I sure did enjoy this afternoon."

Emmy smiled and noticed a group of children in the distance. "I'm glad," she said. "I hope your classmates will soon feel the same. In the meantime, thank you for your obedience and I'll make sure you don't suffer for their folly. It's time to return to class."

Emmy started her spelling lesson. A few minutes in, she heard footsteps in the hallway. She ignored the interruption and continued teaching. The students looked surprised when she didn't say anything about how late they were. Fortunately, they had the sense to sit quietly and pay attention. Timothy didn't return until the very end of class. He wore a proud smirk.

"Timothy, please stand at your desk and spell absence," she said when he reached his desk.

Timothy's smile disappeared, but he faced her and spelled, "A-B-um-S-I-N-S."

"Incorrect. Take your seat. Frances, please stand and spell absence," she said. Five more students spelled the word incorrectly until Sheila stood and spelled the word for the class. Emmy continued teaching spelling and dictation until the end of the day. Just before she rang the bell, she stood to address the class.

"Class, I have some news." Several students scrunched their brows. "Many of you missed our arithmetic lesson this afternoon. You were one hour late for school and you now owe me one hour of your afternoon."

Murmurs erupted. "My Dad expects me for chores," John said.

"I need to baby-sit my little sister," Maria shouted.

"I've got piano lessons," said Felicity.

Emmy held up a hand to supress their disapproval. "You chose to be late," she said. "Any time you miss without permission from your parents or me will be owed at the end of the day. You will have to explain to your parents why you were late for your other obligations. Emily and Sheila, you may go home." Then she rang the bell, said goodbye to Emily and Sheila and began her arithmetic lesson again.

# CHAPTER FOURTEEN

*Home Visit*

Emmy took great satisfaction in her challenging job. Her class was beginning to mind her. They never skipped class after that first day, but they were still noisy and rambunctious, especially in the hallway. Their penmanship was illegible, and their reading improved so slowly Emmy wondered if they heard anything she said.

Timothy, however, was the worst. He still called out in class, threw spitballs when no one was looking, bullied other children in the school yard and missed many days of school. She suspected these missed days were not all necessary. Her methods of detentions and lost privileges did not seem to affect him. It was time for the next step.

Emmy set off after breakfast on a Saturday morning. She had made house calls before, but always as a courtesy, rather than an intervention. She had planned to tell Timothy on Friday that she would be visiting his home and to pass on the information to his parents, but he was truant and so she set off, without assurance anyone would be home to receive her.

There was hard snow on the ground, but the sun was shining on the chill morning. Emmy dressed warmly and had bread and cheese in her pocket for the way home, in case she wasn't treated with the usual prairie hospitality. She suspected a boy like Timothy had a rougher home life than most.

Even at a brisk pace, it took her an hour to reach the Kuypers farm by foot. They must be at the very edge of the school district, which was organized so no child had to walk more than four miles to school. On cold days, this must be a hardship for Timothy. He never came by horse.

The unpainted farmhouse was small and there was no fence to mark the property. This would make gardening and keeping chickens or pigs impossible. Emmy couldn't tell how well the fields were tended under the blanket of snow. She heard children's voices and discovered a bunch of them piled on top of Timothy to the West side of the house.

"Hello," she said.

"Who's there?" said a young boy from the top of the pile. He had rosy cheeks, a worn toque and only one mitten.

Timothy looked out from under the pile. "Miss Bennett? Scatter, bugs, this here's my teacher."

The children giggled and tumbled off the older boy, staring up at Emmy.

"Hello Timothy. I'm paying a visit to your family. Is this a good time?"

Timothy looked first pleased and then worried. "Is everything alright? Did I do something bad?"

Five pairs of round eyes studied her. Emmy chose her words with care. "No, I've come to meet your family."

Timothy scrunched his eyes, pondered a moment and then nodded his head. "You came all this way." He shook his head. "No teacher never did that before." Emmy resisted the urge to correct his grammar.

"These are my brothers and sister." He gestured to the children around him. "Matthew, Mark, Luke and this is Sally."

Emmy greeted them. "I haven't seen any of you at school."

"We're too little," Sally said.

"I can start next year," said Matthew, puffing out his chest.

"I wanna go," said Mark. "Did you come to tell Ma I can go too?"

Emmy chuckled. "I'm sorry, I can't change the rules, but I'm pleased you're excited to start. You'll be in school before you know it."

"Come inside," Timothy motioned with his arms toward the house. "The rest of you, stay outside. Don't bug Ma."

The children complained but heeded their older brother while he escorted Emmy to the house. "I can't be long. They'll get into mischief if I'm not watchin' 'em."

Emmy waited, apprehensive, as Timothy strode up the drooping wooden steps and turned the rusted door handle. Screek, it yelled into the chill November air. His little brothers and sister waited on the lawn like Russian stacking dolls arranged from shortest to tallest. They peered at Emmy, then turned their faces away to blush.

"I'll get Mother," Timothy said over his shoulder. "Come on in."

She followed him into the faded house. There was no lamp lit, but the grey morning light filtered through small, dirty windows revealing a sunken, floral couch, a ratty armchair, and a rickety table too small for anything but the tiniest tea tray. Dust clung to every surface and Emmy stilled a sneeze with her mittened hand. The thick dust created a muted hush.

The doorway off the living room led to a plain kitchen. There was a worn patch on the plywood floor, where the family must pass each day to and from their meals. Even from a distance, it was easy to see that none of the kitchen chairs matched. Somewhere, the dull march of a clock beat at the stillness.

Emmy reached to remove her velvet hat, unpinning it from her glossy curls. As she did, Timothy's mother appeared from the dim interior. She was well-advanced in pregnancy and looked disheveled, as if she'd just woken. Despite her crumpled dress, mussed blond hair and slouched socks, she had a warm smile. Her grey eyes sparkled with the same lively spirit as Timothy's.

"Good morning," she said. "If it's still morning?" She laughed at herself and gazed at Timothy, who kissed her cheek.

"Still morning." He grinned. "I'll make tea."

Timothy's mother shuffled toward Emmy and held out her hand. "I'm Opal." Emmy shook her hand and introduced herself.

"Come have a seat," Opal said and led Emmy to the parlour.

"Are the babies okay?" She searched the room for her other children.

"I see them out the window," Timothy said. "They'll be alright a few minutes. Then I'll head back out, if that's okay with you?" He turned his gaze to Emmy.

"Of course. I'm sorry to keep you from them."

"It's okay. Gives me a break." Timothy disappeared into the kitchen and Emmy heard splashing water and clanking dishes.

"He takes good care of you," Emmy said.

Opal's eyes filled with tears, though she still smiled. "I don't know what I'd do without my Timmy. You see, his father died when Timmy was just a baby."

Emmy felt a chill at their similar beginnings.

"I was beside myself and we moved in with my sister. She had six young children herself and I'm afraid I neglected my boy because I was so sad." She reached into her apron for a handkerchief and wiped her eyes.

"My sister didn't pay him much attention and he had to fend for himself. When I finally pulled myself together, he was already four and used to getting his own supper and helping with the chores.

"I swore I'd do better and then I met Ben," She sighed and glanced up at a photograph on the fireplace mantle. "Such a handsome man with a good heart."

Timothy carefully balanced the tea tray as he came into the parlour and set it deftly upon the table before them.

"Thank you," Emmy said. "You've done a fine job."

"You're welcome Miss. If you don't need me anymore, I'll go back outside."

Emmy nodded, and Timothy kissed his mother once more before he shot out the door like a released criminal. Emmy offered to pour, and Opal accepted, leaning back into her chair and stretching her back, with closed eyes.

"We moved to this house as soon as we married. Ben hoped to farm, but of course, farming's been terrible." She opened her eyes to accept a cup of tea.

"He started going door to door, selling anything he could. Now, he's enlisted in the war. Meanwhile, I kept getting in the family way." Her cheeks reddened.

"You have beautiful children." Emmy tried to cover her embarrassment.

"They're sweet and I love them, but when I'm with child, I get so ill. I have no energy and I'm useless around the house."

"Timothy takes care of you all, then," Emmy said as much to herself as to Opal.

Opal's face crumpled. "I know he should be at school, but some days we need him. I send him as often as I can. Is that why you've come? Is he trouble at school?"

Emmy hesitated. All the things she'd planned to say seemed cruel. "I didn't understand," she said. "I wanted to make sure you knew he wasn't at school. I didn't realize his many responsibilities."

"I'm sorry," Opal said. "I should have written a note. I thought Miss Miller knew and would tell you."

Emmy smiled, hoping to reassure her. "Well, now I know and perhaps I could make up some school work for him to do at home. Things he could do with the other children."

Opal smiled, but her eyes had lost their glitter. She looked like she needed to lie down.

"He's had to learn to be entertaining," she said. "It's how he survived at my sister's, making the other children laugh so they'd notice him. I hope he's not a bother."

Emmy shook her head. "Perhaps I can find some way to use his talents in the classroom. Do you think he'd like to be in the Christmas play?"

"Oh yes." Opal sat up, her eyes glowing. "What a wonderful idea. And he has the most angelic voice, if you need anyone to sing."

"That would be grand." Emmy swallowed the

rest of her tea and stood. "I'll clear this away before I go. Thank you for having me."

"Thank you," Opal said, her eyes half closed.

Emmy took the dishes to the kitchen and washed and dried the cups and saucers. Opal was sleeping in her chair when Emmy returned for her coat and hat. She left the house, pulling the door closed quietly behind her.

Outside, Timothy and his siblings clustered round her. "Was everything alright?" Timothy asked, his eyes full of concern.

"Yes, very good. The tea was excellent. Your mother is sleeping now."

"Mama's so tired." Sally shook her golden hair.

"Yes, you're all doing very well to let her rest. Timothy, I told your mother I'd like to give you a part in the Christmas play. You can practice at home whenever you can't make it to school. I'd also planning to make you a work booklet to do at home on the days your mother needs you. What do you think of that?"

Timothy beamed. "That's real swell, Miss. I'd like that very much."

"Very well then." Emmy smiled back. "It was nice to meet you all and I hope to see you back at school as soon as you can."

"Yes, Miss," Timothy said. She said goodbye and turned back home.

Timothy's school attendance did not increase sub-
stantially; however, he did all the homework she
sent home and became much more enjoyable in
class. Whenever he came to school, Emmy made
sure to have him read aloud. He added sound effects
and read with great expression. He also learned his
lines faster than anyone else in the Christmas play.

# CHAPTER FIFTEEN

*Christmas Concert*

After a biting cold end to November, the children were restless and tired in December. Emmy thought it best to begin preparing the Christmas Concert. They wrote Christmas stories and held votes to decide which ones should be read. Emmy decided they would write the Christmas play together, to draw the most they could from the experience. The older students took turns reading the Christmas Carol while other students copied out the parts they wanted to read.

In Fanny's classroom, Mary Drummond helped collect costumes from previous years. White angels, fuzzy sheep, shepherd staffs and a wooden manger were stored in a corner of the classroom. They also learned Christmas songs and made paper snowflakes and chains.

On the third week in December, Mr. Blaine arrived with a spindly tree from his property. He even broke into a smile as he gathered the oldest boys to help him place it at the front of Fanny's room. Emmy tried to keep the children sedate and working on grammar, but even Mr. Blaine didn't seem to expect complete silence at such an exciting time. He stayed to watch the younger children string popcorn and hang their paper snowflakes on the tree.

"I'll bring the candles on the night of the Christmas concert. I have a collection from previous years in my workshop," he said and left.

The children returned to their preparations for the concert with even more fervour. The tree was a symbol of the concert's imminence and importance.

The concert was to be held on the Saturday before Christmas holidays. Emmy woke that morning to rattling windows and a whiteout.

Snow was up to the windows in the farmhouse and the fire took constant attention to stay lit. The storm showed no sign of letting up. Emmy kept looking out the window. At noon, it was clear that the concert could not go ahead as planned. Mr. Blaine, despite the weather, was working in the barn. She could see the attraction as the children grew whiny and housebound. He trudged into the house for lunch, his mustache covered in icicles.

After he had stomped his boots outside and peeled off his layers of work clothes, he sat before the fire and lit his pipe. The children were momentarily occupied by a puzzle and so Emmy approached him.

"Mr. Blaine, the storm has not let up all morning and the snow is growing very high. I believe with these bitter winds and conditions we must cancel the concert. I would like to request your permission to go to Mrs. Drummond's home to make some phone calls."

Mr. Blaine peered at her in his disconcerting manner. Was he judging her appearance or her character? He rocked a moment before answering.

"The concert will go ahead as planned. We've never cancelled before and there's no need to cancel now due to a little female unease."

Emmy's skin pricked with anger. How dare he blame this on her sex!

He repacked his pipe and lit it again, drawing deeply. Then he smiled. "A bit of nerves should be expected for your first concert, I should think, Miss Bennett. You can't use a little snow to avoid something you find fearful.

Emmy cleared her throat and clenched her fists. "I have all the confidence in the world that the children will put on a concert of high quality. All my fears lie in the danger they must face in order to travel to the school." Then she turned on her heel and strode past the Blaine children to her bedroom. The children had grown eerily quiet. They'd likely heard every word between her and their father.

Unfortunately, she couldn't stay seething in her room. Mrs. Blaine announced that lunch was ready no less than five minutes later. Emmy closed her eyes, pressing her fingers into them and forced herself to open her door and join the family for lunch.

At 5 p.m., Mrs. Drummond appeared at the Blaine's door.

"Good evening," she greeted Mrs. Blaine once she'd pulled the door closed against the swirling snow. "Miss Bennett was meant to meet us at our home, but I didn't like to leave her walking in this snowstorm," she said, her cheeks glowing red. "Would the older children like to come with us as well? Nothing like a sleigh ride in the snow!"

"They haven't had any supper," Mrs. Blaine said.

"That's no trouble. A little bread and butter should keep up their spirits and there's the night lunch after the concert."

Mrs. Blaine looked to her husband for guidance and he nodded once. Then there was a flurry of activity while the seven school-aged children dressed in coats, hats, mitts and scarves and their mother buttered a loaf of bread. She also pulled several foot warming stones out of the stove to be placed beneath flannel blankets for the ride. Emmy was impressed with how quickly the children were ready and pleased she wouldn't be walking alone in the storm. Mr. Blaine, his wife and the youngest children would come later in their horse and buggy.

Emmy forgot her fears of travelling in the blizzard when the children started singing Christmas carols accompanied by sleigh bells. Mr. Drummond added his deep baritone voice to the mix and they glided through the snow. They arrived at the school house before 6 o'clock, giving Mr. Drummond plenty of time to stable the horses. The boys started the stove properly. Mr. Blaine had sent the candles for the Christmas tree and Emmy and the girls put them into place. The result was a warm and inviting school house just in time for the other families to arrive.

At five to seven, the rest of the Blaine family had not appeared.

"Where's Mommy?" Cassie asked, pulling on Emmy's dress. "I want her to see me."

Emmy smoothed the girl's blond braids. "I'm sure they'll be here as soon as they can."


Fanny's classroom was to be used for the concert, where Mr. Blaine had installed the tree the day before. There were too many students to fit into the one hot and stuffy room, which smelled of egg salad. Instead, each class waited in another classroom until it was their turn to perform. Emmy waited with her buzzing class of 30 burgeoning teenagers, trying to keep them quiet.

"Timothy, could you do something?" Emmy said after shushing her class for what seemed the one hundredth time. Their part in the concert wasn't until closer to the end. The younger children began with their songs and recitations while her class grew more and more boisterous.

Timothy looked pleased with the request and gathered the class with his mysterious charisma into a circle on the floor. His hair, usually dull and matted, gleamed gold in the lantern light as he told a ghost story in a low hush. His classmates leaned in to catch every word. Emmy took a calming breath and strained to hear his wonderful tale.

There was a knock at the door, just as Timothy finished. "It's your turn," said one of Mel's students in a loud whisper. The spell was broken, and the children leapt to their feet. "It's my debut," Timothy said to Emmy. It had been one of their vocabulary words that week.

"Break a leg." She grinned and led her class to Fanny's classroom. It was their first chance to see the lights and decorations. They seemed to shrink before Emmy's eyes into scared little children when only a moment ago they'd seemed a large, unmanageable mass. Timothy pushed past the nerves and tremors and introduced their piece.

"Long ago, in Jolly Ol' England, there lived a miserly gentleman by the name of Ebeneezer Scrooge," Timothy said in a commanding British accent.

The assembled parents and other friends and families burst into applause at the familiar introduction. Emmy perched on the seat reserved for the teacher at the front, ready to prompt any student who might need assistance. Emmy turned and saw Maria, frozen on the stage. She glanced at her notes and read out the prompt. "Christmas is the time for sharing and forgiving." Maria shook herself from her fog and said the lines, her shoulders relaxing with each word until she smiled.

The play continued without another prompt. They received a standing ovation at the end, which Emmy knew was entirely due to Timothy's performance. Eventually, Emmy gathered her class into their little room so Mel's class could perform.

After getting her class to promise silence, she opened their door a crack so they could watch the upper class recite 'Twas the Night Before Christmas. She noticed her students melt into their younger selves and could almost see the sugar plums dancing through heads. After the senior class finished, all the students gathered in the hallway to sing Silent Night. The schoolhouse felt full and holy; wrapped in peace in a time of war.

Still, Mr. and Mrs. Blaine and their little children were missing. Emmy's mind filled with dread, but she was distracted from her worries by jingling bells. A portly man dress as Santa Claus made his way to the front of the room.

"Ho, ho, ho! Merry Christmas!" he said. "I hear there are many deserving children in our midst. Ho, ho, ho! Come and get your Christmas treats!"

The children lined up in surprising order while Santa passed out candy canes. Emmy recognized Mr. Drummond behind the white beard. The Drummond family must have bought candy for all the children. Emmy knew this would be the only gift some of her students would receive this Christmas.

Mrs. Drummond appeared at Emmy's elbow

and pressed an envelope into her hands. "Merry Christmas, my dear. I'm sorry it isn't more. I hope this will help you have a good Christmas at home." She hugged Emmy and smiled.

"Thank you," Emmy was embarrassed by the stiffness in her voice. She wasn't accustomed to monetary gifts. She had hoped to earn her way, rather than becoming a charity case. As much as she wanted to return the envelope, she couldn't go home empty-handed.

After the concert, there was a night lunch of cookies, sandwiches and watery tea. Emmy tucked into the meal with relish after only a piece of buttered bread several hours ago. Fortunately, Cassie was taken up with the food and excitement, but Emmy knew there would be questions later.

Despite frigid temperatures, all the children except Sam fell asleep on the sleigh ride home. He sat stiffly on the bench in front of Emmy and she wondered if he knew that only the direst of circumstances could keep his father from attending the school Christmas concert.

When they arrived at the Blaine property, Mr. Drummond insisted his wife stay beneath the coverings while he helped carry Cassie into the house. "Something's up," muttered Mary.

"Best if you stay with the children," he replied, patting her knee. "Miss Bennett, please lead the way," he said before Tommy or George could cut in front of her. She nodded in the darkness and led the sleepy crew into the dark farmhouse. When she opened the door, it was nearly as cold inside as it was out. "Hurry children," she instructed. "Gather the coal and wood. I need to restart the stove. She bustled about, fighting panic in order to find and light the candles. She carried a lantern through the house while the oldest boys worked on the fire. Cassie whimpered from her spot on the ragged sofa. Emmy noticed the Blaine's bedroom door was closed. She knocked. "Mr. Blaine? Mrs. Blaine?" There was a low moan within and Emmy pushed the door open.

Mrs. Blaine was huddled under the blankets with the two youngest fast asleep beside her.

"Mrs. Blaine?" Emmy whispered, afraid to wake the children. "Millie, can you come out?"

The woman shook her head, but then gasped a sob and covered her mouth. She untangled herself from the blankets without disturbing the children. Then she followed Emmy to the kitchen where Mr. Drummond had helped the boys start the fire.

"There you are now, there's your mother."

Mrs. Blaine stood before them, as if frozen. Then her chin trembled, and she collapsed into the nearest chair, dropping her head into her arms. "He's dead," she wailed. "Dead! Died in the snow. . . Trying to get . . . to the . . . concert." She hiccupped and sobbed. Emmy reached for the nearest coat and wrapped it around the woman's frail shoulders. Her skin was icy and Emmy hurried to check the babies but they were warm in their sleep, wrapped many times in knitted blankets. At least Millie had the sense for that.

When she returned to the kitchen, she was relieved to see Mrs. Drummond and her children.

"It's too dangerous to go for the doctor right now. Why didn't we cancel the Christmas concert?" she shook her head.

Emmy knew exactly why.

Shortly after, Mr. Drummond took Sam and Tommy out to find their father. Mrs. Blaine seemed especially concerned her husband was left out in the snow. Emmy offered to help.

"No, no, my girl," Mr. Drummond pushed away her offer. "You stay in and take care of the little 'uns. We need you here."

Later, Emmy learned the buggy was still in the farm yard where Mr. Blaine had tried to push it out of the waist-deep snow. Mr. Drummond and the boys loaded Mr. Blaine's body into the Drummond's horse carriage and brought him into the barn.

Mrs. Drummond was fixing tea and a plate of sandwiches left over from the school lunch. Emmy coaxed the children into putting on their pajamas and cleaning their teeth. Then she tucked them in and kissed their heads, soothing their brows as they sobbed. But they were too tired to cry for long. A simple blessing.

When she returned to the kitchen, Mrs. Drummond whispered that Mr. Blaine's body was secured in the barn and covered in blankets. Mr. Drummond would fetch the doctor as soon as it was safe to do so. The Drummonds would stay the night, huddled together on the floor in the living room.

"You can have my room," Emmy said. "I'll sleep with the children."

"That's kind of you," Mary patted her arm. "We best stay with our children. They'll probably be waking in the night. This is all terribly upsetting. We've slept on floors before. It's no great burden."

Emmy felt guilty to have a bed and room all to herself, but when she lay down in her nightgown, all thoughts disappeared. She sunk into a heavy sleep.

The morning dawned clear and bright and it was as if the blizzard the previous night could have been a mere nightmare, but when Dr. Alberts arrived, the nightmare was confirmed.

"It looks like a heart attack," he said in the kitchen. He sipped at a cup of tea after examining his patient. "I'm so sorry, Millie. He was a pillar of our community."

Mrs. Blaine sat in the rocking chair wrapped in blankets before the fire. She still hadn't warmed, and Emmy whispered to the doctor her fear of shock.

"She won't be the first," he said, shaking his head. "Make sure she eats and drinks and gets a little exercise. Will the children be able to help?"

Emmy gazed at Sam and Tommy with their heads lowered. They'd already been out to feed the chickens and check on the damage done by the blizzard.

"They're good children. But they're only children. They can't be expected to cope."

Dr. Alberts stood to put on his coat. "That's just what they'll have to do, I'm afraid. Like it or not, the children will grow up ahead of their time."

He doffed his hat on his way out but spared the boys by asking Mr. Drummond to help him load the body into his carriage. He'd explained to Mrs. Blaine that her husband's remains would be properly stored until the ground thawed. The funeral would be held at the church on Monday. Emmy would be back in Shelby by then, missing the entire ceremony.

# CHAPTER SIXTEEN

*Home*

The bus pulled into Shelby at three in the afternoon on December 19. Main Street was decorated with Christmas banners and lights in the shop windows. Emotion welled in Emmy's throat, threatening to break into a sob.

Two of her sisters waved as the bus pulled into the station. Emmy was relieved to get out of the stinking behemoth. A drunken man had started the trip several seats ahead of her and Bev but moved back to sit in the seat across from them. She had stared firmly ahead the whole time, fighting the urge to nod off. Bev had fallen asleep the moment they left Harding and was oblivious to their imminent danger. She woke when the bus stop, hugged Emmy and said, "I'll see you at church!" before running off to greet her waiting family.

"My Emmy," her mother embraced Emmy while her siblings gathered around, waiting their turn.

"Did you bring me something?" said Becky, wrapped in Emmy's old wool coat.

"And who are you again?" Emmy said, pretending not to recognize her growing sister.

"Emmy!" Becky's eyes filled with worry.

Emmy squeezed her shoulders. "I could never forget you, my darling. Even if I were gone for 100 years."

Her stepfather met them at the wagon. "Ah, there's our little worker bee. Tell us how much you made, then." She ignored his request and stepped into the carriage, but he grabbed her arm.

"That's no way to treat your elders," he said. "How much did you make?"

Emmy whipped her head around to see who might be watching this scene, but the street was empty. "I'll not speak of this in public," she said. "Wait until we get home."

"Ach, let her go now." Her mother gently patted her husband. "We'll get this all sorted at home. Kiss your father hello, Emmy."

Emmy pursed her lips, but obeyed her mother, kissing his stubbly, dry cheek. He grunted but released her. She settled in the far corner of the buggy, her cheeks burning.

Once home, her mother fetched tea and cake and her stepfather returned to his question.

"You know, Emmy, we've provided for you all this time. Will you not share your earnings with your family?"

"Owen," her mother started, but he glared at her and she stopped.

Emmy cleared her throat. "I would be more than happy to share my income. It was my intention all along." She stared at her worn sleeve. "However, the Harding school board has also suffered from the Depression. I have made $200."

Her stepfather snorted. "I find that hard to believe. Teachers made twice as much as that when I was a child."

Emmy's face grew hot with rage and shame. "Then search my bags," she stood and opened her arms wide. "They gave me some money to buy a Christmas present for my family and that is all." Her voice was too loud. She dared not look at her mother.

Her stepfather stood so he would not be at the disadvantage of height.

"So, you've wasted yourself then," he said. "When you could have been helping at home."

"What more do you want me to do? I cannot demand what they do not have."

Her stepfather glared at her, his face turning purple. He stomped from the room into the parlour.

Emmy was shaking with emotion. Her mother touched her hand and Emmy whipped her head around, ready to argue. But she saw her mother's face was gentle, filled with love and empathy.

"There's nothing I can do, mother," Emmy sunk into a wooden chair.

"There, there, girl. "We're all suffering. It's no one's fault."

Emmy's ire and shame were soothed by the presence of her brothers, sisters and her mother. Her stepfather took her earnings and stayed away. At last she could relax and put her feet up. She told her siblings about the Christmas concert without mentioning Mr. Blaine. She would tell her mother about him later, once the children were in bed.

"I played the part of Mary this year," Becky said when Emmy finished her tale.

"She tripped over the Baby Jesus," said their brother Jack.

"Did not! I never fell, just wavered a moment."

"How is that any different from tripping?" said Gordon.

Emmy tried not to laugh. "I'm sure you were the model of decorum. Your teacher made an excellent choice."

"Jim played the accordion," said Mary. "Howard the fiddle and Jack sang. It was swell!"

"I could use a little cheering up myself," said Emmy. "Would you show me what I missed?"

Her mother brought tea and settled beside her eldest daughter while the younger children scurried about for props, instruments and costumes. By the time they poured the second cup, the children were arranged and began an abbreviated version of the concert.

"This is where Joseph would have said 'We are not worthy of thee, my Lord,' to the angel," said Becky.

"I'm not sure that part's in the Bible," whispered her mother. "It seemed a bit more creative this year."

Emmy hid her smile behind her napkin.

They enjoyed a cozy week together, interspersed with the grumblings and complaints of Emmy's stepfather. When he was home, the children subdued themselves and worked quietly on indoor pursuits, or, more often, struck out for the frigid outdoors to skate, toboggan or snowshoe. Emmy was grateful for the respite from her duties and responsibilities as teacher but couldn't help reflecting that being the eldest of nine children was strikingly similar to being a teacher. She took advantage of the extra license to tease.

One frosty afternoon, Emmy caught her mother alone, folding laundry in her bedroom. Pale light filtered through the frosted window. A cross-stitched Bible verse was the only wall decoration. Her mother's few beauty implements; a comb, brush and face powder, lay atop a crocheted doily beneath a small, pocked mirror. Emmy pulled the bell-shaped pendant from its hiding place within her dress. "Mother, why did you never tell me you were a teacher?" she asked.

Her mother paused mid-fold and froze. Emmy worried she'd gone too far. They rarely spoke of personal matters.

Then, her mother sighed. "I suppose I gave you the necklace, so you would ask." She finished folding the shirt and patted her bed, so they could sit together.

"I was desperate for money after your father

died," she gazed into the past. "I thought it would be better if you grew up in a family, so I left you with my sister-in-law. I told myself they loved you as much as I did." Tears glittered in her eyes.

"There were so many schools popping up, they needed teachers almost as badly as I needed money." She smoothed her dress. "I gave my maiden name. They didn't ask much. I taught the fall term, staying with a different family every week. . ." Her voice drifted while her face twisted through a myriad of emotions. Emmy waited.

"It was dreadful, being away from you. I couldn't ever mention I was a widow. Yet, I loved the children. The teaching kept me from running back to you." She gazed at her daughter. "How did you enjoy teaching?"

Emmy smiled. "The children are lovely."

Her mother nodded once. "Yes. After four months, I couldn't continue. I gave up my post and returned to you. I gave all the money I earned to my in-laws so they could keep us until I found a husband. A father for you." Her mother stood and returned to her folding. Emmy joined her, lost in imagining what it would be like to teach while your child was left alone.

On Christmas Eve, their family piled into the buggy with extra blankets and foot warmers. A full moon filled the sky and lit the snow and Becky snuggled into Emmy for extra warmth.

The children started singing Jingle Bells; Jack's

voice was changing and could alternate between soprano and bass at times, causing much merriment along the way. Until their father had enough.

"Silence," he bellowed. "You're botherin' the horses. Hold your tongues. We'll have enough singing at church." They obeyed but couldn't help passing funny faces when Owen's back was turned. They stopped when their mother gave them a stern look.

The windows of the little white church glowed with warm candle light, beckoning them inside where it smelled of damp wool and wet leather. They shook hands with the usher and gathered along their pew, the one her natural father had purchased for before he passed away. Before their mother became a poor widow, weak to the first eligible suitor. Emmy's eyes traced the familiar engraving. Dedicated to the glory of our Lord by Henry and Jean Bennett. Her stepfather simply claimed the pew as his right, never offering to donate the money to have his own bench.

Emmy shook off her mean thoughts in the spirit of Christmas and lost herself in the carols.

"Oh, little town of Bethlehem,

How still we see thee lie."

It was both comforting and stifling to be right back in the church she'd grown up in. Would she ever spend a Christmas elsewhere? She looked at her sister's beaming face and wondered if that was really what she wanted.

Their heads were bowed in prayer when there was a shuffling at the door. Emmy fought the urge to turn and look – she had years of remonstrance for such offences, but Becky was not as well trained.

"Emmy look!" She pulled on Emmy's sleeve.

"Hush now," Emmy said.

"But Emmy." There was an excited whine to her little sister's voice. Emmy heard others shuffling and whispering and then even the minister stopped his droning prayer. One of the women squealed "My son!" and Emmy at last gave in.

There, at the back of the church, dressed in uniforms of varying good fit, stood a row of soldiers three men thick.

"Hallelujah!" shouted the minister "Welcome home. Won't you join us for our closing hymn."

The men disbursed to join their families, hugging and kissing them as they went. Howard and Harry joined Emmy's family and their pew grew tight once more. Emmy's heart was already full to bursting when Lars approached and took her hands in both of his. She remembered holding his hand the last time she had seen him. "Happy New Year," he said in his slow way. Emmy squeezed his hand hard, hoping to squeeze back her tears as she did, but there was no need. Tears shone in every eye in the church and at last, the organist struck the chord and they sang together,

*"Rejoice, the Lor♦ is King:*
*Your Lor♦ an♦ King a♦ore!*
*Rejoice, give thanks an♦ sing,*
*An♦ triumph evermore.*
*Lift up your heart,*
*Lift up your voice!*
*Rejoice, again I say, rejoice!"*

Emmy was certain the entire church had never meant it more.

At the end of the song, there was one final prayer and at last, all the families could embrace. Howard grabbed Emmy and gave her such a squeeze she gasped.

"What's going on?" she said, breathless when he let her go.

"The brass at the army base gave us some time off for Christmas and New Year's. They'll be shipping out some of the men in January, but for now, they thought it was best if we all went home. It will save them cooking us Christmas dinner."

Emmy gazed at Lars, standing nearby, wishing she could embrace him as well.

Lars seemed to understand her gaze. "They let us come by train. We couldn't make it in time for the start of the service so one of the guys suggested we organize a sneak attack."

Emmy's high laughter rang above the rest of the din. She smiled all her feelings onto Lars. "What a lovely surprise."

Parishioners gathered in the tiny church hall after the service to share tea and Christmas baking. Her mother had brought a Christmas cake. It was meagre this year, as it had been the past few years; hardly any fruit or brandy and much smaller, but still a Christmas cake. Her younger siblings probably didn't remember how rich Christmas cake once was.

Before he even had a chance to get some cake, Lars had pulled his brother over to Emmy.

Emmy waited with an encouraging smile while Lars found the courage to speak.

"Earl, this is Emmy Bennett. We met at camp this summer." He managed to say at last.

Earl's eyes sparkled with mirth. "The schoolteacher, yes. I remember you mentioned her once or twice." He cocked an eyebrow at his brother, as if threatening to say more. "How was your first term?"

A hundred memories came to mind, challenging, joyful, frustrating and sad. "It went well, thank you. What brings you to town?"

"Even trappers need a Christmas," he replied.

Miraculously, Emmy's curious younger brothers and sisters were occupied with friends and sweets, so she was able to speak with the two men for several minutes without interruption.

"I took in over one hundred pelts this season," Earl was saying. "Still bring in a pretty penny. Gave me enough to take the train in for Christmas. Our mother was happy to see us."

"Who buys the fur?" Emmy asked.

"Americans and Europeans, mostly," Earl replied. "There's still people rich enough to buy fur, believe it or not. Seems a shame to steal it from the Canadians. We're the ones who need the warm coats in the winter. I think the Brits and the French wear it more for looks.

"During the coronation of King Edward VIII in '36, there was such a demand for fur, a man chartered a plane to see us and bought our catch for $900. That was a good year."

All too soon, Emmy's stepfather broke up their conversation. "Time to get back in the buggy," he said. "Little ones are tired." He stomped away.

Emmy's cheeks reddened. "Merry Christmas." As she stepped away, her heart sinking, Lars piped up behind her. "Do you curl, Miss Bennett?" She turned to see his twinkling eyes and smiled.

"I do, Mr. Callas," she said.

"Can I take you to the New Year's Bonspiel?" he said, staring at his toes.

"I'd like that.,"

"You can bring your brother," Earl nodded at Howard, who was approaching.

"Evening, Callas," Howard nodded.

"What do you think, Howard? Should we have Earl and Lars as our curling team?"

Howard sized up first Earl and then Lars. "Callas is a good man. Steady. I'd like that." The men shook hands and Lars winked at her when no one was looking.


There was a foot of new snow to greet them Christmas morning. Emmy snuck her Christmas presents to the living room while it was still dark. She placed the little gifts beneath the tree and then stole quietly into the kitchen to start breakfast. There was an orange for each child, which she placed around the table. She gave hers to her mother. Then she boiled water for tea.

Becky woke first and burst into the kitchen with wide, excited eyes. "Oh Emmy, I thought this year the tree would be empty, but there are presents!" she whispered.

Emmy hugged her sister and kissed her cheek. "Have you given up believing in Santa Claus?"

Becky shrugged. "It's more that I hope in him, rather than believe." Her little sister looked much older for a moment, but then she gasped. "Oranges, Emmy!" she pressed her hands together under her chin. Emmy was pleased she had been able to defer the aging of her sister, at least for the day.

The other children trickled into the kitchen, followed by their mother. "Happy Christmas, children," she whispered, and they gathered around to receive their Christmas kisses. She turned to help with breakfast, but Emmy wouldn't allow it.

"Everything is well in hand, Mother," she said. "Becky and Mary will help me. Why don't you peel your orange?"

"Oh no, Emmy." She held the golden orb to her eldest daughter. Emmy pressed her mother's hand away.

"There's no mistake. Santa left this one for you."

Tears welled in her mother's eyes, but she accepted the gift and peeled the orange slowly, inhaling the citrusy scent and savouring each section.

It was nearly ten when her stepfather woke and they could sit down to enjoy their proper Scottish breakfast, albeit considerably smaller than the breakfast she remembered as a child. It was the one day a year her mother insisted on the splurge.

"God we thank Thee for Thy bounty. Amen," said her stepfather.

A small bowl of oatmeal and cup of tea sat before each family member and they tucked in with zeal. They were used to having their breakfast much earlier.

"Did you eat well with your host family?" Howard asked once their bowls were wiped clean and Emmy and Mary brought out the toast.

"Well enough," said Emmy. "They are . . .were also a family of eleven, plus me, so we were conservative in meals, but never went hungry." She still had not told them Mr. Blaine had passed away. Maybe if she didn't tell them, it wouldn't be true.

After toast, there was an egg, scoop of beans, sausage, broiled tomato, scone and a thin slice of blood pudding for everyone. When she was a girl, there was bacon as well, but this was extravagance enough. Various murmurs of appreciation and enjoyment passed around the table, although Becky and Mary turned up their noses at the pudding. Emmy waited to catch their eyes and gave them a stern look – it was her mother's favourite and she would not let her sisters spoil it with their Canadian tastes. They lowered their heads and dutifully ate their round black slice.

The children were old enough to have learned that no presents would be opened until the last dish had been washed and put away, but Becky, the youngest, didn't like it.

"No other family has to wait so long," she said.

When, at last, the kitchen was spotless, they moved into the living room. Her older brothers looked like pickles squeezed into a jar in the tiny parlour. They lit the candles and set a fire in the fireplace. Then each child under twelve received a new pair of socks with a few candies from Santa. Next, Emmy gave a candy stick to every person in her family and her mother gave those older than twelve a new pair of knitted socks that looked mysteriously similar to the ones from Santa Claus. Her stepfather excused himself. Emmy was pleased he was gone when she presented her gift to her mother. She withdrew an envelop from her apron pocket and placed it in her mother's hand.

"What's this, my dear? You've already given your gifts." Her mother smiled.

"I'm a working woman now, mother. I wanted to spoil you just a bit."

Her mother opened the envelope without damaging it in the least. Then she read the enclosed card and her eyes widened. "Oh Emmy, this is too much."

"It's for the whole family to enjoy." Emmy placed her hand on her mother's shoulder. On the card were instructions for the delivery of new kitchen linoleum. Her brothers or stepfather would need to install the linoleum, but she was pleased to offer her mother a replacement for their patchy, damaged kitchen floor which she knew was a source of great embarrassment.

Emmy leaned down to receive a kiss from her mother and a pat on her cheek as well. "Thank you, my dear. You're everything a mother could hope for."

There was a pared down Christmas dinner with turkey, potatoes and a small Christmas cake. After supper, her stepfather returned to his workshop. The rest of the family played charades until midnight and went to bed filled with the goodness of Christmas spirit.

# CHAPTER SEVENTEEN

*Disappointment*

Emmy lay her dresses on her bed and ranked them based on wear, colour and practicality for curling. It was the afternoon before New Year's Eve and butterflies danced in her stomach as she prepared for her date with Lars. If only she had the money to buy herself something new, but she shook off the useless wish and switched her flower print for her more practical tweed suit. Flowers were for summer, after all.

Becky knocked before flinging herself into Emmy's room.

"Emmy, can't you take us sledding? The sun's up and the fields are calling."

Emmy chuckled at her sister's childish exuberance. She would have scolded her other siblings for such an entrance, but she couldn't reprimand the youngest.

"First, tell me what I should wear tonight," she

said, resting a hand on Becky's shoulder.

"This one!" Becky pointed to the thin white cotton dress Emmy bought two years earlier for a cousin's wedding.

Emmy looked heavenward. "I should have known better." She reached for the flowery dress and returned it to the closet. "That's a summer dress, Becky. It's the dead of winter. Now, which would you choose?"

Becky scowled and bit her lip. "But that's the prettiest. You want to look pretty, don't you? Jean says you're meeting a fella."

Emmy's eyes widened and Becky giggled. "I suppose I have no secrets in this house. I don't need to freeze myself to impress any man."

"Is he the tall man? From church?" Becky said, eyes shining. How did she always know so much?

Emmy nodded.

"He's awfully tall, Emmy. You'd best wear your highest heels in case he wants to reach down and kiss you."

"I never!" Emmy reached out to tickle Becky who squealed and zipped out of the room. Served her right for asking a child. She kept out the tweed and replaced the other worn dress in the closet.

Lars arrived with Earl. They were both dressed for the weather and wore fur caps. She wished she had something as warm but made do with what she wore to and from school.

Her stepfather trapped the two young men at the door.

"You boys come for our Emmy?" he asked.

"Yes sir," replied Earl.

"You'll have her back by 11 p.m. and no later," Owen puffed out his chest. Although he heavily outweighed the brothers, he was at least a foot shorter.

"Yes sir," Earl repeated.

"What are you still trapping these days?" They had only thirty minutes until the bonspiel began, but there was no avoiding her stepfather's interrogation.

Earl answered in the same clipped fashion. "Beaver, mink, muskrat, fox. It's the best we can do during these hard times. My brother and I were at it four years, though he's up and joined the army now. I'm doing my best to hold down the fort."

"Isn't winter the best time for your work?"

Earl only whistled and studied the ceiling, forcing Lars to speak up.

"The Indian folk can last all year in the bush. They're used to it," he stared at the floor. "We miss the warmth of company, especially this time of year." He turned to his brother who nodded. Emmy's stepfather narrowed his eyes.

Lars dropped his voice to a whisper, his eyes darted to Becky who was trying her best to eavesdrop. "It's best to avoid the cabin fever, sir." He peered at his brother once more. "We saw a man succumb to it last year. Didn't want Earl to catch it."

Emmy wasn't sure what cabin fever was and, it seemed, neither did her stepfather. The strangeness of the statement put an end to his questioning. Emmy and her brother Howard grasped the opportunity to join the Callas brothers and clamour out the door.

No matter how long Emmy lived on the bald prairies, she could never get used to the shock of cold of a frigid winter night. She rubbed her hands together and tried to steady her breathing, hurrying to keep up with the long-legged brothers.

"I'm sorry there's no car to transport you, Miss Bennett," said Lars.

Emmy's laughter froze and shattered like broken glass in the still night. "No one drives a car these days, Mr. Callas. Who can afford it?" She tried to keep her voice light, but she worried her legs might freeze again.

Earl grumbled. "It's this dang Depression, pardon my language," he said. "We were born at the wrong time. We should have lived when our parents were young and there was money in farming, instead of struggling to survive in the North."

Emmy was surprised at the darkness in Earl's statement.

"Aren't you fond of your life?" she inquired.

Lars answered. "It has its good parts, sure enough. But it's hard work and it wears on a man."

Emmy shivered. "I'm sure I couldn't endure it. I love to curl and dance."

She caught Lars's admiring expression in the moonlight.

"And well you should," Earl shook off the darkness and turned magnanimous. "A pretty young thing like yourself would be wasted in the barren north."

Emmy was pleased to note they arrived on time, despite her father's interview. "Emmy!" sang out a light, high voice through the din. A moment later, Bev grasped her in a tight hug.

"Bev!" she gasped. "It's so good to see you!"

Her round smiling friend released her from her bear hug. "I was sick as a dog after Christmas. Just got out of bed today. Thought I might die."

Emmy linked her arm through her friend's and drew her into a quiet corner.

"Have you heard anything from Harding?" Emmy inquired.

Bev sighed. "Nothing. I do wonder how the Blaine's are doing. I pray for them every night."

Howard interrupted to announce their team was set and to squeeze Bev's hand. Emmy kissed her friend's cheek and pulled her brother to join Lars and Earl on a sheet of ice.

The ice sheets were set in an old barn. It kept out the wind, but little else. Still, Emmy knew from experience that the exercise would soon warm her chilled feet and legs.

"Harry tells us you're a fine curler," Lars drawled. "We signed you up as skip."

Emmy smiled, but felt a tingle of dread. She hadn't played all winter. What if her skills forsook her?

"I hope you won't be disappointed," she said.

Harry draped his arm over her shoulder. "Not you, sis. You're a star."

Their team won the coin toss and chose to throw the first stone. "Lars, can you take lead?" Emmy asked and he assented. "Aim for the front of the blue circle," Emmy instructed. "We'll want some guards." Then she slid down to the end to strategize and oversee their efforts. She pointed to the spot on the ice and Lars nodded.

Howard and Earl stood ready to sweep. Lars tipped the rock to wipe it clean and then tested its weight along the ice. Emmy could tell he'd played before. She studied his aim.

"Sweep!" she called into the echoing rink. Earl and Howard swept the rock straight down the cen-tre of the ice, but Emmy knew the slight spin would place the rock exactly as she'd directed.

She pointed out the same guard position on the opposite side of the house and was pleased that their team was well set to receive the opposing team's rocks.

After the first round, their team still had one rock in the house, close to the button. Earl played second and she directed him to hit out their oppo-nent's rock. He chose instead to go straight for the button, knocking their guard out of the way and leaving them with no rocks in the house.

"Sorry about that," Lars grimaced. "My brother likes to go his own way."

"I see," Emmy said through pursed lips. "Any recommendations?

Lars grinned. "You might try telling him to do

213

the opposite of what you want. It should work for you, but I think he's on to me."

Emmy chuckled and nodded once, then pointed her broom away from their opponent's rock. Sure enough, Earl hit their rock out, leaving his own in its place as guard.

Howard threw well and when it was her turn, she felt confident their team could win. Howard directed her as she would have done and after the other team's skip took the final turn, they scored three points.

"One down, nine to go," Earl announced.

As the game continued, Emmy noticed how Lars covered for and protected his brother. He seemed more like the older brother than the younger. In her family, as the oldest of nine, she was always the steady, responsible sibling. It was strange to see things done another way.

In the end, their team outscored the other by twelve points. They shook hands and gathered around the tea urn.

"How much longer can you stay home?" Emmy asked Lars while they nibbled on cookies.

"Our leave ends tomorrow," he said. "I'll go back to training and my brother will go back up north. That's when trapping gets profitable."

"Doesn't your mother miss you?" she asked.

Lars laughed. "I reckon she gets enough of us in a week. We don't usually stay home for long. Earl and I are used to doing our own thing, so we travel around, visiting family and friends, helping out where we can. I figure she hopes we'll settle down one day." He stole a peek at Emmy.

"She probably wishes we'd start a farm of our own, but farming's become a fool's errand. Costs more money to start than you can get out. Heck, I know of at least a dozen farms I could take for free. Nobody wants them anymore. I don't suppose you would consider being a trapper's wife?" Lars finally looked at her intently.

"Heavens no!" Emmy blurted. "It's cold enough here in the winter. I suffered frostbite this winter. Besides, what would I do all day with no one to talk to but the wolves?" Emmy stopped to look at Lars. His shoulders drooped and he was staring at his shoes again.

Emmy's cheeks heated. Lars wasn't asking out of friendly interest. She tried to take the edge off her previous statement. "Do many women live up north with their husbands?"

"There are a few," Lars muttered. "You're right, though. It's no place for a cultured lady like yourself. I'm going to get some more tea."

Emmy couldn't think of a way to fix what she'd said. He hadn't actually asked her to marry him and yet she could tell her answer had offended him.

When it came time to countdown to midnight, she received a hug from Howard, but Lars was nowhere to be found. She hadn't realized she was hoping for a New Years' kiss.

Emmy escaped to the kitchen, under the guise of cleaning up the tea. It was a tiny, cramped room with a little stove and cupboards for dishes. She was carefully washing the teacups in a bucket of water, heated on the stove when she heard a shuffling behind her. Emmy hastily wiped her tears with the back of her hand. Then Lars's hand was on her shoulder, pulling her close. She leaned into him.

"It's just the worst timing." She let him lift her chin to meet his gaze.

"There's never a good time for war, Em. The longer I know you, the harder it will be to leave you."

He gazed into her eyes and though she wanted him to kiss her she looked away. She could lose her job. She felt a tear run down her cheek, which he caught by his thumb. "I'll cherish this," he said, studying the glistening drop.

She swatted him and laughed despite herself. They held one another and for once, Emmy didn't care who saw them.

They eventually separated, and Emmy returned to her task.

"Well, now we have to pay for our embraces," she said after dipping her hands into the water. "The water's barely warm enough for washing."

Lars reached for the dishrag and took over washing. "This is how you'll always remember me," he joked handing Emmy a glistening cup to dry. Emmy shook her head. She studied his warm blue eyes, aquiline nose and full lips. What if she forgot his face? She placed the dried cup in the cupboard.

"Just a minute," she said and hurried to the hall, finding Bev standing a little too close to Howard.

"Bev, could you take a photo?" she asked, suddenly shy.

Bev blinked as if she were coming back from another world. Then she smiled. "Of course. Give me a minute."

Emmy found her camera and grasped Bev's hand.

"Where do you want the photo to be taken?" she asked.

Emmy surveyed their meagre surroundings, shabby through the eye of a camera. "I guess the sofa will have to do. It's too dark outside."

They arranged lamps and cushions until Emmy was satisfied and she sat, smiling, beside Lars.

"Here goes," said Bev. She did her best, but her nervous hands blurred the photo, which would remain locked inside the camera until Emmy could afford to have it developed.

"If I write, will you write back?" Lars asked just before he dropped her and Howard back home.

"Of course," Emmy said, and hurried inside before she started crying again.


Howard and Lars left the next day, as did many of the men in the community. Emmy stood in the kitchen with her mother, watching her brother grow smaller as he rode off with a group of friends. Even Mary and Jean hoped to join.

Emmy's mother was scrubbing laundry with

vigour. "It's terrible, Emmy, to hear them talk about how they hope the war will last so they can see some action. They try to do it out of my hearing, knowing how much I hate it, but you know how unaware they are. I hear them whispering. How can I tell them what terrors await?"

Her mother had never spoken so passionately. Usually they talked about the weather and house-work. Only something truly horrid could so un-hinge her mother's tongue.

# CHAPTER EIGHTEEN

*Second Term*

School was cancelled in January, due to the cold. While she waited to return to Harding, Emmy oversaw the installation of linoleum in her mother's kitchen, helped with the cooking and cleaning, taught and read with her younger siblings during the daytime and played cribbage, Euchre and Crokinole with her older siblings in the evenings. Although these activities kept her comfortably busy during the day she worried about Lars and her brothers at night. She was anxious to return to her classroom in the hopes that life would seem normal again. At least Mrs. Drummond's weekly letters kept Emmy informed.

I think, dear Emmy, you will be as sad as I am to hear the Blaine children have been split up amongst friends and relations. All of Mrs. Blaine's family died in the 1920's flu epidemic and Mr. Blaine's family is small. They took the oldest three, the baby and Mrs. Blaine, but the middle five were left to be divided. I wanted to have all five, but we have only Frank Junior and Cassie.

I don't want you to worry about where you will be lodging. Mr. Drummond and I would be pleased to have you. We can offer you your own room. You're welcome to ride to school with the children and Mr. Drummond or me. We drive them during the coldest days.

We haven't yet chosen a replacement for Mr. Blaine on the school board, but I'll let you know once it is settled. We are meeting this Thursday night to decide.

The children and I will check on the school before you return. We don't want you to worry about dust or mice. I look forward to having you back. January is always dull, and I know you'll help brighten the dark months.

All the best to you and yours. Happy New Year, too.

Emmy wrote back immediately, accepting Mary's kind offer. She looked forward to the situation. She was saddened by the news of the Blaine family, especially the separation of the younger children. All the more reason to get back to school where the children could at lease see one another.

Bev started visiting every second day.

"Have you heard anything from Howard?" She always dropped this question into the conversation at some point. Emmy smiled. She would love to have Bev as a sister-in-law.

"Nothing since last week," Emmy said as she

EMMY IN HARDING

pulled another stitch through the sock she was darning.

Bev sighed. "I'm starting to feel an old maid. What if there are no men left after this war and we end up teaching the rest of our lives, stuck at home in January when it's too cold even to teach?"

"Are you ready to retire already? I'm in no hurry," Emmy said and snipped the thread. "We have the rest of our lives to be married."

"Men can be married without giving up their jobs. It's so unfair."

Emmy agreed, but there was no use stewing over the way things were. She dealt a hand of cribbage and they abandoned serious talk for the rest of the afternoon.

Despite the cold, Emmy's family bundled up for church that Sunday. With the two oldest boys away, they had more room in the wagon, but Emmy would trade all the room in the world for the warmth of her two oldest brothers at her sides.

The hot bricks at their feet seemed to cool instantly and did nothing for the biting wind in their faces. Emmy wrapped an arm around Becky, who whimpered on occasion, as much to keep her sister warm as herself. But the pink morning light on the crusted snow and stiff, leafless trees was stunning. Emmy wondered if her brothers and Lars could see the same brilliant sunrise.

The other families in the community had also risked the cold to come to church. Being stuck indoors so long made the chance to meet with others a treat. It took a few minutes extra for their minister to get them to stop talking so he could begin the service. Emmy always found January services dull after the exuberance of Christmas carols. Her mind kept wandering to Christmas Eve and the surprise arrival of Lars and Howard. After the fifth time telling herself to focus on the service she gave in and allowed herself to pray for their safety and health instead. If one could not listen at church, at least one could pray.

Emmy and Bev had kept aside enough money to return to Harding by bus at the end of the month. They wanted no repeat of the long tedious journey by horse and cart they'd experienced that autumn with Mr. Blaine. It was still frightfully cold, and though the bus was protected from the elements, it didn't offer much warmth. Emmy was glad for the warming brick her mother sent along.

"I feel like I've forgotten to teach, being away so long," Bev said as they huddled together.

"I'm certain everything will come back to us," Emmy said, though she felt a nervous twinge in her belly.

Mary met them at the bus station with her daughter Florence and Cassie Blaine. Emmy's eyes filled with tears.

"You both look so grown up!" she exclaimed. The two girls wore new winter coats. She hugged them all and tried to brush away her tears, unseen.

No need to remind Cassie of her father's death.

"Mr. and Mrs. Drummond gave me this coat for Christmas," Cassie grinned, revealing a missing tooth.

"It looks very smart," Emmy brushed a snow-flake from the girl's shoulder. How could her mother have left her, so frail and impressionable? She caught Mrs. Drummond's full eyes and knew Cassie was well-loved in her new home.

"How was your journey?" Mary said as she let them to her horse and buggy.

"It's so quick by bus," Bev said.

"The stops along the way that slow you down, but still less than two hours," said Emmy.

"You'll be glad to get home and settled," Mary helped them store their cases and then expertly drove them to their lodgings.

"Goodbye Miss Lafferty!" Cassie and Florence waved to Bev.

"I'll see you tomorrow morning at school," Emmy said.

There was a roast, potatoes and carrots for supper at the Drummonds. Mary's cooking was as good as Emmy's mother's and she ate until she was full. Cassie sat by her side and was intent on filling her in on every moment she'd missed over the holidays.

"William got a new sled and we went out almost every day to the hill nearby." Her blue eyes shone.

"Is that so?" Emmy asked. "Hasn't it been cold?"

"Frightfully so," Cassie replied. "I nearly lost my

cheek to frostbite." She'd never been allowed to talk so freely at her family's table.

"Not quite," her brother corrected her. "She just had a small circle of white. We got home in plenty of time."

"But it still turns red when I sneeze," Cassie interrupted.

"Why don't we give Mr. and Mrs. Drummond a turn to speak," Emmy said.

"Not at all," smiled Mr. Drummond. She'd never seen him so contented. "It's a pleasure to have our house filled with conversation," he smiled at his wife. "They've had a good break together."

The Drummonds would not allow her to help with the dishes after supper on her first night, so she played charades with William, Frank, Arthur and Howard in the parlour while Cassie and Florence helped Mary tidy up.

Emmy had two days to prepare for the second school term. William and Arthur accompanied her to the schoolhouse to start the fire, sweep and shovel. Their help saved her and Bev at least two hours of work and allowed them to concentrate on organizing their lessons. Bev had learned they could send away to the school board in Regina to request copies of plays and music for the spring concert. This would save them from writing everything themselves. Bev drafted a letter to the school board requesting several plays to be mailed for consideration.

The students returned to school rested and eager to learn. They had lost some of their stamina for seat work, so Emmy made sure to give extra time for exercise and fresh air. The cold snap let up for the first week and the children were anxious to enjoy the great outdoors. She asked the children to bring in a variety of seeds to attract winter birds and they studied animal tracks they found around the school.

They made Valentine's cards out of whatever leftover paper they could find. They also wrote Valentine stories and memorized poems of love and friendship.

Emmy found her own Valentine surprise in the mail. It was a red heart cut by hand and decorated with a variety of hand drawn birds and flowers. It read:

"Dear Emmy. I've taken the liberty of writing you at your school. I often think about our time together on New Year's Eve. I miss your lively smile. In admiration, Lars."

Her cheeks flushed as she read the card in her room. She tucked it into her book for safe keeping and allowed herself to reread the card once a day before she went to bed.

She began corresponding regularly with Lars. It took several weeks for letters to get back and forth, but he seemed eager to reply and so she had several letters a month. Besides looking forward to getting to know him better, Lars's letters were rich with fascinating memories about living in the North. She asked if she could read excerpts to her class and his letters grew even longer. On a dull March morning, she read:

"We owned a four-dog team which is the usual number for a white trapper, although occasionally a man will drive three or five dogs. With them we transported our gear: bedroll, axe, rifle, traps, bait, and grub box, and other essentials for life on the winter trail that often includes a tent and small stove. They haul the heavy loads of meat from where we shoot it, often out of hilly, difficult terrain where a great deal of energy must be used up by both the driver and his dogs before reaching the cabin."

Emmy's students loved hearing about Lars and Earl's dogs, Snuff, Duke, Meg and Cap. She told Lars as much and so his letters always included something about his team. Some of her students were so inspired by Lars's tales that they asked to write to him. He answered each letter individually. Emmy worried over the expense of the paper, but the inspiration it provided some of her most reluctant writers was priceless.

She brought up the cost of postage and paper at her next board meeting, which now included Mr. Hamm. To begin the meeting, they offered up a prayer for the Blaine family and Mary Drummond gave a warm speech of Mr. Blaine's legacy to the school, the community and his family. Emmy was impressed Mary could make such a stern and unlikeable man sound like a model citizen and father.

Of course, her own feelings toward the man had softened upon his death. Perhaps it was natural.

They voted Mr. Purdy as School Board President, although it was clear Mary was several times more suited to the position. Having a woman on board at all was an anomaly. On paper, it was technically Mr. Drummond who had the board position, but at the beginning of each meeting, she was approved as his proxy. They added Mr. Hamm as Vice-President.

When the question of money for postage and paper arose, Mr. Purdy asserted some authority.

"I have heard my girls joking that this Mr. Callas is a beau of yours, Miss Bennett," he said without looking at her.

Emmy willed herself not to blush.

"Is there any truth in that statement?"

"No, Mr. Purdy," she answered.

"I trust you remember your contract forbids you from entering into an engagement to marry for the duration."

"Yes, sir," she said through gritted teeth.

Mrs. Drummond cut in. "Our boys have spoken fondly of Mr. Callas's letters. They can't wait to hear more about his adventures. Thank you, Miss Bennett for introducing them to this remarkable way of life."

Emmy pursed her lips and nodded.

"You must know, Mr. Purdy, how children, especially girls, like to arrange every young, single person in marriage. I recommend you nip the gossip in the bud. There's no reason to embarrass

Miss Bennett. She's carrying out her duties beyond reproach."

Mr. Purdy flinched as if he'd been struck. Somehow, Mary Drummond could say what others could not.

"Of course," he said drily. "Thank you for your advice. A father is not always as wise to the way of girls as a mother would be." His eyes shone too brightly, and Mrs. Drummond patted his arm.

"You're doing a wonderful job. Your girls are lovely."

They approved the provision of postage and paper for letter-writing and then discussed the upcoming spring dance and visit by the school inspector. "The Day The Inspector Comes" was something Emmy remembered from her own experience as a student. The experience as a teacher was even more frightening. She listened carefully to what the Board advised, making notes about the date and her responsibilities.

"The board will come in the weekend before to make sure the schoolhouse is in ship shape," Mary said. They divided the jobs of window cleaning, floor scrubbing, general maintenance and wall-washing amongst themselves.

"Please keep a list of any needed repairs," Mr. Hamm said.

Fortunately, the visit would not be until May, so there was plenty of time for the school dance before the Inspector came to call.

# CHAPTER NINETEEN

*Spring Dance*

Looking over the children's progress for February and the beginning of March, Emmy was impressed by how much they had learned since she started with them. Their penmanship, arithmetic and reading were coming along, and Emily, Sheila and Bertrum were already working on the next grade. However, once spring thaw began, attendance fell off.

"I can't say Mr. Blaine didn't warn me," she said to herself after taking attendance on a warm morning at the end of the month.

Satisfied that her students were still on track to completing their work for the year, she turned her focus from the three R's to preparing for the spring concert and dance. The plays from Regina arrived. Emmy felt she could have written better material, but she was growing weary and it was nice to have one less task. She chose the story of Goldilocks and the Three Bears. It was much simpler than The War of the Worlds, which she looked back on as quite a feat of effort and imagination. The children, already familiar with the tale of Goldilocks, were much quicker to learn their lines and so they had more time to practice songs and poetry. This turned out to be a blessing with all of the absenteeism.

"I've written about Mr. Callas's dogs," William said to her a week before the concert. "Could you please check it over?"

William rarely approached Emmy for help or correction. She silently thanked Lars for inspiring such bravery.

"Of course!" She smiled.

*Little Meg, the only girl,*
*Came to camp as the winter snows swirle•.*
*Small Snuff came next,*
*Light brown an• mighty*
*Pulling the sleigh*
*An• lea•ing the others.*
*Cap an• Duke*
*The Labra•or-Husky pups*
*Coul•n't be more •ifferent*
*In temperament.*
*Cap, like a bear,*
*Coul• carry a man on his shoul•ers*
*While Duke le• the team*
*Into every kin• of trouble*
*From shirking his •uties*
*To starting night howls,*
*He woul• have been shot*
*If he ha•n't looke• so noble.*
*How I'• love to run with these •ogs*
*Through the sparkling snows*
*Of the white Cana•ian North.*

William must have pored over Lars's descriptions of his four sled dogs. It had affected him deeply and Emmy's throat caught at what it revealed about William's difficult year.

"It's perfect, William," Emmy said. "Would you consider reciting it at our concert?

William blushed and didn't answer right away. She carried on assisting and teaching the other students until he returned to her side. "I'll do it, Miss. If you think it's good enough."

"It certainly is," she encouraged him. "Thank you. It will add so much to our program."

Practicing for the spring concert had additional benefits. Children badgered their parents to let them attend school so they could get better parts in the concert. Since the play was relatively easy to learn, Emmy dedicated the morning before recess to cramming in as much schoolwork as possible. The students grumbled, but when she threatened to continue seatwork until lunch, they stopped complaining and put their heads down.

The evening of the concert was mild and sunny and Emmy couldn't help comparing it to the deadly Christmas concert blizzard. Mrs. Blaine attended looking even weaker and paler than before. Emmy shook her hand and thanked her for coming.

Emmy's head felt as fizzy as soda, but she forced herself to focus on the task ahead. The children opened the concert in spring song. They looked bright and sweet in starched outfits and combed hair. Their smiles invited the audience in and Emmy's heart filled with pride over their accomplishments. She had worried over their poor rehearsal earlier in the day, but all the previous mistakes were forgotten as the students performed to their best ability. The evening ended with William's poem and Emmy stole glances at his mother as he recited. His normally quiet voice was strong and unwavering in the close schoolhouse. She heard every word. Mrs. Blaine's eyes twinkled with tears, but then she brushed them away and resumed her stoic watching.

Mr. Hamm took advantage of the excited applause to start the bidding for the Box Social. Emmy ushered the children off the little stage and nearly missed the bidding for her own box. She'd done her best to bake cakes and make sandwiches that afternoon, but her mind had been preoccupied with the concert. A wave of exhaustion swept over her before she realized her little lunchbox was bringing in higher and higher bids.

"Sold to Mr. Purdy for $1.50. Thank you for your generous donation, Mr. Purdy. You'll be sharing your lunch with . . ." Mr. Hamm paused for effect. "Miss Bennett! Congratulations and have a lovely evening." Mr. Hamm raised his eyebrows and the crowd broke into murmurs and whispers. Mr. Purdy strode to the front to collect his winnings and then marched toward Emmy.

"What a bit of luck," he said to her with a tight-lipped smile.

Emmy heard giggles behind her and wished any man but Mr. Purdy had bought her box. Had he somehow known it was hers? She remembered seeing young men eying boxes as they were placed on the little table at the front.

"Thank you, Mr. Purdy," was all she said. She resumed returning children to their parents as the bidding continued.

There were twelve box lunches and they brought in $7.75. She saw Bev eating with Timothy, Emmy's student. With the war on, the younger boys had been allowed to bid on behalf of their families. Perhaps Emmy should be glad she was sitting with a man, rather than a student.

It was a good income, all things considered, and the couples wandered off to eat together on tables or in the school yard while the other guests helped themselves to a table of sandwiches and goodies.

Emmy watched Mr. Purdy gather up the courage to speak as she nibbled on a scone. "You did a wonderful job with the children tonight," Mr. Purdy said, at last. She smiled but did not wish to encourage him.

"Your girls have sweet voices," she said.

"They're very fond of you," his voice grew deep.

She would have returned the compliment but worried he would take it the wrong way.

"I believe you square dance," Mr. Purdy said near the end of their meal.

Emmy nodded. She'd never said so little.

"Please save the first dance for me." He stood to brush the crumbs from his lap.

"I will," she replied. "Thank you."

Mr. Purdy gathered up the litter from the box. "Your lunch was delicious. Thank you. Although I prefer less mustard, for future reference."

Then he turned and took the litter to the bin. Emmy shook off the restraint she'd been harnessing while in his presence.

Emmy visited with parents and students until it was time to dance. The caller took his place with the fiddler and Mr. Purdy suddenly appeared at her side. They joined the other dancers. Those who weren't dancing gathered around the school walls and clapped in time to the music.

Emmy tried her hardest not to be embarrassed by Mr. Purdy's poor musicality and inability to follow dance instructions. "Over here, Mr. Purdy," she said, more than once. She felt her face flushing but hoped it would be attributed to the exercise. She curtseyed with gusto when the song was over, pleased to be free of her obligations.

"You're an energetic dancer," Mr. Purdy said. "Admirable."

"Thank you," Emmy nodded. She accepted all other offers to dance, avoiding Mr. Purdy for the rest of the evening.

When the food and punch were finished, and the fiddler played his last song, Emmy and Mrs. Drummond gathered the remaining children to help tidy the room. Mr. Drummond and several other fathers carried the desks back into place. It was after midnight when they emerged from the schoolhouse into the cool night.

"A great success," proclaimed Mrs. Drummond. "We raised more money tonight than in the past three years."

"That's wonderful, Mary." Emmy smiled. Her body ached and her head rang with loud music and conversation, but it felt good to have a job well done. Mr. Drummond drove them home and Emmy tried her best to stay awake while the children dozed off. She looked forward to the day of rest before her.

# CHAPTER TWENTY

*Visit to Callas House*

Lars and Emmy's brother Howard were given five days leave in April, which gave them just enough time to get home for a day before heading back to Ontario. Howard collected Bev and Emmy in Lars's buggy. It was a three-hour drive to Red Lily, but it felt much shorter. Emmy basked in the freedom of being on the road. They pulled into the Callas farm just past noon. The farmhouse was small, but neat and all the fences were in good repair. In the distance, they saw Lars whittling on the front stoop, but he jumped up to meet them as they drove in.

"Good day," Howard raised his hat when Lars approached.

"It just got better." Lars smiled. "Follow me. We'll let the horses rest in the barn. I've got it all ready."

Howard, Bev and Emmy stepped out of the buggy and walked with Lars toward the barn. Halfway there, they met a solid, stout woman with a wispy white bun knotted on top of her head. She wore a long apron over a dark dress. The apron was sprinkled with blood and she carried an ax in one hand.

"You are the Bennett siblings," she said in a thick accent.

"Only I'm a Bennett. My brother's surname is Stanwick and this is my friend, Bev Lafferty," Emmy said.

"Eh?" Mrs. Callas said.

"Mother's just butchered a chicken for dinner." Lars chuckled. "She insists on doing it herself."

"Thank you for having us," said Bev.

"My boys can't be trusted. They're used to the wild animals. These domestic chickens need a woman's hand."

Mrs. Callas wiped her rough hand on her apron and held it out to Emmy.

"I'm sure it will be delicious," Emmy said, accepting the woman's blood-spattered hand.

They settled the horse into the barn and Lars led them to the water pump.

"Sorry about that," Lars said. "Mother's from the old country. She thinks fine manners are a waste of time."

Howard laughed. "She's a real spitfire, Lars. I like her."

After washing, they went to the kitchen where Lars served tea and scones. "We have a late dinner, Sunday. I thought you might be hungry after your journey."

There was a shuffling in the hallway and Lars bolted from his seat. "Earl," he said, blanching, and hurrying out of the room.

Howard's forehead crinkled in confusion and

Emmy wondered why Lars was so worried about Earl.

There were hushed voices and the sound of a tussle. Then a door closed, and Lars returned, disheveled.

"My apologies," he said, his full lips pulled into a thin line. "Earl is better off in bed. He's not up for company."

"It's fine," Emmy said. "We're in his house. There's no reason for him to hide."

Lars' face crumpled an instant, but his mother banged through the door, a plucked chicken in each hand and he shook off the emotion.

"Lars, you going to cook these, or do I have to do everything around here?"

Lars took the poultry from his mother. "I'm all ready, mother. Have some tea and put your feet up."

"Feet up, pah. I haven't done that in sixty years." She disappeared down the hallway.

Emmy stood to help Lars, but he assured her everything was under control and insisted Howard, Bev and Emmy have another cup of tea and help themselves to the playing cards.

"Don't mind if I do." Howard shuffled and dealt a hand of cribbage.

Halfway through the game, Lars put the chicken in the stove and his mother returned in a clean dress and smoothed hair.

"Card games, yes. The young should play games. Good." She sat heavily upon a kitchen chair, grunting.

"Would you like to play?" Howard asked. "We

could start again?"

"Not me," she poured herself a cup of tea. "I'll watch."

"Fifteen two, Fifteen four, pair for six. . ." Emmy counted, feeling self-conscious about Mrs. Callas' close inspection.

"Humph. Good with numbers. That'll serve you," she muttered.

They played to the finish and Emmy won by twelve points.

Howard grinned. "My brilliant sister. No way to beat her."

"You need to pay more attention, boy," Mrs. Callas said. "You kept giving her points in the kitty. You need to use your noggin'." Mrs. Callas tapped her temple.

"Too true, Mrs. Callas." Howard laughed.

Suddenly, there was a banging in the hallway. Lars leaped up, but Earl stomped into the kitchen before he could be stopped.

"Laughter," he said, his eyes roving around the room. His hair stood out from his head. He was dressed in wrinkled pajamas. "How can you be laughing?"

"Earl, I think it would be best. . ." Lars began, placing a firm hand on his brother's shoulder. Earl twisted himself out of reach.

"I've had enough of listening to what is best. I can't stay in there any longer."

"Earl, we have guests. Go get dressed," his mother said.

Earl clenched his fists, but turned and said "Yes,

mother."

Lars watched him go. "I'm sorry," he said.

"It's alright, Pal. Can't be good for a fella to stay in his room all day."

Lars sighed and wiped his hand over his eyes.

"My son has not been right since he returned from the bush," Mrs. Callas said, her eyes distant. "I should never have let him go."

Lars placed a hand on his mother's shoulder. "He wanted to go, mother. These things happen."

Earl returned, still in his pajamas. He held a hunting rifle. "I'm off," he said. "Can't stay in here gabbing like women. Gotta work." He shuffled out the door. Emmy could see Lars wanted to stop him.

"The doctor says it's cabin fever. We're supposed to keep him calm," Lars said. "But that only seems to make it worse."

Emmy couldn't help comparing this discontent, unsociable Earl with the charming, vibrant Earl she first met at church. "Does the doctor think he'll overcome the cabin fever?" Emmy asked.

"He'll get better," Mrs. Callas nodded her head repeatedly. "The Callases are a hardy breed."

The chicken was ready shortly afterward and they ate their meal in solemn contemplation. Emmy imagined they were offering up silent prayers for Earl with every fortifying mouthful.

Earl did not return before they needed to head back home. Mrs. Callas shooed the young people outside so she could wash the dishes. The two couples paired up for a walk down the dusty country road. Emmy knelt to pet the soft fur of an early purple crocus peeking up through the ditch. She waited until Howard and Bev were far enough ahead to allow for some privacy before she stood.

"My students sure love your letters," Emmy said after walking several minutes in silence. There was too much to say and no time to say it. The gentle wind passing through the brown grasses sounded lonely to Emmy.

"What about you Emmy? Should I keep writing to you too?" Lars' face was drawn.

Emmy stopped to look up at him. "Of course. I love your letters even more than they do." She made sure no one saw them before she allowed herself to lean her head against his chest. She felt him kiss the top of her head.

"Will you be shipping off soon?" she asked, her voice muffled in his sweater. Canadian Geese cried out above them.

"Next month, they say."

Emmy took a long shuddering breath and allowed Lars to press his lips against hers. When she opened her eyes to make sure no one had seen them, she saw he was smiling widely.

"What are you thinking of, Lars Callas?"

"Wouldn't you like to know."

Emmy shook her head and swatted him playfully. "You're daft." He caught her hand and brought it to his lips. She let him a moment and then pulled it back.

"That's enough now."

"Yes ma'am," Lars tipped his hat at her and she laughed.

# CHAPTER TWENTY-ONE

*Inspection*

"Thank goodness," muttered Mrs. Drummond on a rainy May morning as she read the newspaper. "Winston Churchill is the new Prime Minister in Britain. He's just what we need."

Normally, Emmy would have asked for more information, but it was the morning the Inspector would come and she couldn't concentrate on anything but the school day before her.

She'd stayed up late, poring over lesson plans she'd written up in excruciating detail. Before leaving the previous day, she'd used her best handwriting to scribe the day's lessons on the blackboards and put fresh flowers in a mason jar on her desk.

Emmy did her best to protect her head from the rain with a scarf and arrived early, but the Inspector was already there. He was smartly dressed in a suit, coat and tie, but she noticed his shoes, though polished, were well worn.

"Miss Bennett?" said the white-haired man. He had a kind smile.

"Good morning," she said, shaking his hand.

"I'm Mr. Temple, the school inspector."

"Yes, hello Mr. Temple. We're expecting you. How are you?"

The gentleman nodded. "Well enough, Miss Bennett. It's a grand morning and I was treated to a warm bed and hot breakfast at Mr. Purdy's. His two little girls have already told me about your expert teaching practices."

Emmy's cheeks felt hot and she pulled out her key to open the school. "That's good of them. They're very bright. Would you like to come in?"

Mr. Temple lifted his hat in gratitude and followed her into the schoolhouse.

"I'll just put my hat and bag over here, if that's alright?" Mr. Temple motioned to an empty table at the back of the classroom.

"The children usually place their lunches here," Emmy said. "This bookshelf might work better. You're welcome to use my desk as well."

"Thank you," said Mr. Temple. Emmy hung up her coat and looked over her lessons until Mr. Temple joined her at the front.

"The way I usually conduct an inspection is by going over the day plan with the teacher. Then I look over the grounds, building and privy, and observe your morning lessons."

"Very good," Emmy said.

"If you don't mind, I like to teach the children for an hour before lunch. I know it's a taxing day for young teachers and I like to keep up my own practice."

"They'll enjoy that," Emmy said, surprised. "I'll mark that in my plan."

"I taught for ten years in one room schoolhouses," he said, gazing about the simple room. "It's not for the faint-hearted. I know the effort it takes to be a leader in a strange community. How are you finding it, Miss Bennett?"

"They've been good to me," she said. "I accepted a change in classes in November. One of their teacher's left. It was a bit of a struggle at first."

"Mr. Purdy mentioned the change. How are you finding your host family?"

"The Drummond family has been most hospitable."

Mr. Temple made a note on his papers. "Have you been with the Drummonds the whole time?"

"Just since second term. I was staying with the Blaine family, but Mr. Blaine died tragically just before Christmas."

Mr. Temple looked up from his paper with a pained expression. "Oh dear. How is his family?"

Emmy shrugged. "It's been difficult, of course. They have nine children who have been split up amongst family and friends. Two of them are living with the Drummonds."

Mr. Temple shook his head. "If only our society made it easier for families to stick together in such circumstances. It makes a terrible situation so much worse when they are separated."

He looked over her plans. "Your students are

lucky to have such a thoughtful teacher. I can see why the Purdy girls like you. I'll leave you to your preparations while I look over the grounds. Is there anything I should be aware of?"

"You'll find everything well worn, but in working order. The school board takes care of any problems we bring to their attention. Of course, it would be nice to have a new barn and a fenced yard, but times are hard everywhere and they're doing the best they can."

"Very good," Mr. Temple took up his papers and strolled outside.

The children began to arrive dressed and groomed as if it were the Spring Concert.

"Good morning, Emily. Don't you look smart today!"

"Thank you, Miss," said the tall, dark haired girl. Then she whispered, "I'm a bit nervous. You must be too, but don't worry about a thing. You're the best teacher we've ever had."

Emmy's throat tightened with emotion. She smiled. "Thank you, Emily. You don't need to worry about a thing either." Emmy patted the girl's shoulder. Emily took her seat and arranged her chalk and slate.

Emmys class was surprisingly quiet when Mr. Temple returned with the ringing of the school bell.

"Good morning, class," Emmy said as he strode into the classroom. "Please rise to greet our special guest, Mr. Temple."

The students obeyed and said, "Good morning Mr. Temple."

He walked to the front of the classroom and stood before them. "Thank you for the warm welcome. I hope you won't mind if I take a seat at the back of the classroom for most of the day. I may come around to see your work at some point, but I hope this won't make you nervous."

Timothy Kuyper raised his hand.

"Yes, Timothy," Emmy said, bracing herself for a smart remark.

"Won't you be quizzing us? The other Inspector liked to quiz us on what we know."

Emmy waited for his answer. This was her experience as well.

"I'll be teaching you a bit before lunch and might include a few questions, but I find it's best to see what you're used to first. If I could tell a short story, Miss Bennett?" he looked to Emmy who nodded her head.

"When I was a boy, about your age, the Inspector came to my school. He was tall and scary and when he asked me the capital of Canada, I was so nervous that I said Regina. Of course, I knew it was Ottawa, but all I heard was capital and I answered before I heard the whole question. Back then, teachers weren't as kind as they are today, and I had to stand with the dunce cap for the rest of the class."

There were murmurs of empathy around the class.

"I know an Inspector can make children and even adults uneasy. I'd rather we all have a nice day together."

Emmy felt herself relax and the faces of her students seemed to ease as well.

Mr. Temple took his seat at the back of the room

and after the morning routine of prayers and song, most of the students stopped turning to look at him.

Since it was May and a warm morning, Emmy began by reading The Frog Prince. Her class, she knew, was fond of fairy tales and, after reading the story, went with their slates to look for frogs. She was relieved to find the rain had stopped.

"You must not touch them," she instructed. "If you find one, study it closely. If it stays a while, sit down ever so quietly and do your best to draw it."

The frogs had been loud the past several evenings and mornings. She'd imagined an Inspector might want the children inside reciting, memorizing and quizzing all day, but Mr. Temple seemed pleased to see the children learning about nature and enjoying the lovely morning.

As a child, Emmy and her siblings had often gone frog hunting and she knew it took perseverance and patience. She stayed near Timothy, whom she knew might struggle with being still. Soon all the students found a spot to watch the frogs and seemed engrossed in the project. Mr. Temple drifted from one student to the next, whispering questions and complimenting their diagrams.

When the students had finished their drawings, Emmy called them into a circle to share their work. Suddenly wasps buzzed around their heads and several in her class cried out in alarm.

"Try to stay calm," she said. "They'll leave us

alone if we ignore them."

Instead, more wasps arrived and Frances and Maria screamed every time they got near them. Emmy instructed the class to bring their slates to their desks and take their recess early. They would reconvene to share their pictures and start their writing assignment shortly. She wondered what Mr. Temple must think of such slap dashery, but she could hardly think of him with all the excitement.

Mr. Temple appeared at her side.

"An energetic morning, Miss Bennett," he said with a grin.

"Yes, I'm afraid things didn't go exactly as planned."

"Ah, that is the art of teaching. Being ready for anything. Lessons rarely go as planned."

Emmy returned his smile.

"I'll make note of your good rapport with the students. They truly respect your authority and well-organized classroom and lessons. I'm pleased you took them outside. I would have done the same, but not nearly so well as you did. They knew precisely what was expected of them and became like young naturalists out in the open. So many teachers remain inside, drilling their students while I observe."

"I did wonder if that was expected."

Mr. Temple sighed. "I've considered writing a letter ahead of my visits, to introduce myself and encourage young teachers to experiment with their teaching while I observe. I would rather help teachers iron out the kinks of creative lessons than sit through lecture, drill and practice only to tell them they need to be more adventurous. You were wise to trust your instincts, Miss Bennett. I congratulate you."

Emmy felt a thrill of recognition.

"Now, please, allow me to supervise the students while you take a little break. I know how hard you work and would like to give you a chance to breathe, especially on this stressful day."

It felt strange to leave her students and step inside to make a cup of tea, but she could see there was no use arguing with Mr. Temple and he was soon organizing a game. The children watched him with adoring eyes. She could not take away their opportunity to spend time with an expert teacher.

# CHAPTER TWENTY-TWO

*An Unsolve♦ Problem*

After recess, the students took turns showing their frog diagrams at the front of the classrooms. After sharing, they wiped their slates so they had room to write their own stories, poems or essays about frogs. Emmy gave them 30 minutes to write and then allowed those who wished to read their writing to do so at the front of the classroom. Having a special guest seemed to inspire them.

After the fifth reading, Emmy spoke to the class. "Thank you for your wonderful work. I wish I could keep your stories to read again and again, but now it's time for Mr. Temple's lesson."

Mr. Temple spoke from the back of the classroom. "Please, Miss Bennett. Don't let the children clean their slates yet. Might I suggest they keep their stories for a brief reading period after lunch?"

"Of course," said Emmy, taken aback by his affection for the student's work. She always felt regret when their painstaking words were turned into dust. "Please set your slates to the left-hand sides of your desks."

Mr. Temple crossed the distance from the back of the classroom to the front in a few long strides.

"Thank you, Miss Bennett. I'm keenly impressed with your writing work. I can't wait to hear more. Miss Bennett has been gracious to share her class with me today and I hope you enjoy my mathematics lesson."

Emmy wasn't sure what to do with herself. She stood a moment as he spoke and when he turned to her and smiled, she decided to take his chair at the back of the classroom.

Mr. Temple placed his briefcase on Emmy's desk. He opened it and withdrew a map of the world and a photograph which he set along the chalkboard for all the students to see.

"There is a place called Tibet, here near China," he said, pointing. "There is a large plateau in Tibet and on top are two large rivers. The one in the South is the Yangtze and the one in the North is called the Yellow River."

The students who normally gazed out the window during arithmetic lessons leaned toward the map and seemed mesmerized by the strange sounding words.

"Like the North and South Saskatchewan Rivers?" asked Timothy.

"If you like," Mr. Temple smiled. "A German mathematician named Lothar fell asleep. He was so obsessed with numbers and mathematics that he dreamed about throwing positive integers into the Yellow River. In his dream, mud and silt fell into the water whenever a number hit the water." Mr. Temple pointed to a photograph of a muddy river.

Bertrum said "I used to play by the river and throw rocks to make the mud fall in."

"Ah yes," Mr. Temple said. "If the number was even, it cut the mud in half. If the number was odd, the mud would stick to the number until it grew to one more than triple its size. This continued until it hit the South China Sea." He showed the Sea on the map and wrote a trail of numbers on the board:

$$3 - 10 - 5 - 16 - 8 - 4 - 2 - 1$$

"No matter which number Lothar started with, he ended up at 1."

"My Dad doesn't trust the Germans," Maria murmured.

"The next night, Lothar had a similar dream about the Yangtze. If the number was even, it would halve the mud, if it was odd, it would triple the number and subtract one."

"I've never dreamed in numbers," Frances shook her head.

"Your problem to solve is, Does the Yellow River wear down all numbers to 1?" He wrote this on the board. "And does the Yangtze River wear down all the numbers to 1?" He wrote this question on the board as well. "Yes, Timothy."

"Are you sure this is mathematics? It seems too interesting."

Mr. Temple laughed. "I'm so glad to hear you say that. Please work in partners on the problem. One of them has never been solved."

"Well then how do you think we can solve it?"

Mr. Temple's eyes twinkled. "Ah, that is a good question. I believe young minds are more pliable and original than old minds like mine. Go ahead. Perhaps today you will answer what no adult has yet been able to solve."

There was an excited buzz in the room. Emmy stiffened. Should she quieten them? Mr. Temple seemed to guess her predicament and strode toward her. "Don't worry, Miss Bennett. A little noise never hurt anyone. Take a look." He motioned for Emmy to walk about the room. At first she could hardly keep herself from scolding her students for talking, but then she began to look at their slates and was astounded by their quick sums.

Before dismissing the children for lunch, Mr. Temple addressed the class. "Thank you for your good work today. Although we did not solve the unsolved question, you may continue to work on it in your spare time. If you come to a conclusion, I hope you will write to me. Your teacher has my address."

"I'm so close!" Timothy said.

Mr. Temple grinned. "I hope you will accept this map and photograph as inspiration," he said. "Your teacher may use them as she likes to encourage your mathematical learning." He reached into his briefcase and held up a notebook.

"I would also like to give your class this little book."

The students sat up in wonder.

"Your classroom is full of budding authors. Perhaps you could each contribute your best story to this book. You'll need to draw some straight lines. It would make a nice keepsake. If you like, I can bring a new book each year for such purposes."

Emmy stood, tears threatening. "Thank you, Mr. Temple. That is very generous."

Without prompting, the rest of the class echoed her sentiments.

"You're most welcome. I will return you to Miss Bennett's capable hands."

Emmy took her place at the head of class and dismissed the children by row to collect their lunch pails.

After lunch, Emmy assigned quiet reading while she selected several students to read aloud to her at their desks. A couple of the younger ones had fallen asleep during quiet reading, but when she moved to wake them, Mr. Temple whispered "Let them sleep. It's a long day when the Inspector comes to visit." He winked and Emmy followed his advice.

They woke in time for penmanship and geography and finally a new game outside. Even though Mr. Temple was kind and supportive, she was glad to see the end of the day.

The school board members arrived to review the Inspector's Report. Mr. Temple stole a moment with Emmy before meeting with the others. "I want you to know I've given you an excellent review."

"Thank you, sir."

"You have wonderful classroom management and you're using a good variety of teaching methods. The students are well prepared for their next grades and I hope you will try out at least one lesson in this book."

He passed her a new book bound in red leather. "How should I return this?" she asked.

Mr. Temple held up his hands. "There's no need. Part of my job is to educate and equip our teachers. I only leave books with teachers who are open to learning. Sadly, I've only given out about half a dozen this year."

"Thank you," she said and clutched the book to her chest. "I did have a question about your lesson."

"Yes," he smiled.

"It seemed almost like they weren't doing arithmetic at all. You only spoke a few minutes. How can they learn?"

"Ah, you are observant. We are not the only teachers in the classroom. They also learn from one another and the materials around them. You have done an excellent job of teaching them, Miss Bennett. They are ready for the provocations in this book. You will be amazed at what they can teach you."

Emmy did her best to take in his words. They were at odds with everything she had learned about education.

"Before I meet with your school board, I want to provide you with this reference letter as well. In case you'd like to look for a different situation next year?" He raised an eyebrow.

"I enjoy this school, but I thank you for your letter."

He passed her the letter. "I wish you all the best, Miss Bennett."

Emmy's highest hopes had been surpassed. "Thank you, Mr. Temple. It's been a pleasure."

At the meeting with the school board, Emmy couldn't help wondering what Mr. Blaine would have said about Mr. Temple's suggestions for new readers and a fence around the school yard. Mrs. Drummond assured Mr. Temple they would follow his instructions as soon as possible.

"I know your community has suffered this past decade," he said. "I will be recommending your school for a government grant to cover my recommendations and to provide better wages for your teachers." Only Mary could meet his gaze.

Mr. Temple bid them good day and saddled his horse to visit the next school. He attached an entire camping kit including a bedroll and cooking utensils. Inspectors travelled long distances to visit all the schools in their district. She wished she had offered him tea and biscuits before he set off.

# CHAPTER TWENTY-THREE

*School Picnic*

With the big inspection behind her, Emmy focused on preparing her students for exams, making sure they were ready for the next grade, and writing report cards. She was pleased to see how well the students had done, but slightly dismayed with the numbers of school days missed by some students. Their marks were not as high, but she had done her best, under the circumstances.

Then suddenly, it was the last day of school. Emmy did her best to keep decorum through the morning exercises, but she couldn't reprimand the children for giggling and wiggling through prayers and songs. Instead, she smiled at them, considering this was the last morning they would ever do this together.

After the morning routine, they gathered before

the unlit fire while Emmy read to them from the book Mr. Temple left behind. They had filled it with their stories and poems and now Emmy read the entire book from cover to cover. The students clapped and cheered for each piece.

Timothy raised his hand when they were through.

"Miss Bennett, what will happen to the book now that it's the end of the year?"

Emmy fingered the pages. "I thought we should add it to our library so all future students can read what was written by the class of 1939 - 1940. Would you like that?"

The other students murmured approval. "It's like we published a real book!" said Emily.

Timothy was not satisfied. "That's fine during the school year, but what about the summer? The mice get in here and ruin everything."

Emmy tapped the book and nodded. "I have a lot of brothers and sisters," she said. "Would you mind if I took it home for the summer and read them your stories?"

The class was even more excited. A couple of them whooped and Emmy had to settlethem.

"We'll miss you, Miss Bennett," Timothy said. "I hope they enjoy the stories."

Emmy had to clear her throat from the emotion that threatened.

After sharing the book, Emmy gave each of the students a job in the school or the school yard. She'd never seen them so enthusiastic to clean, but they were pleased to do anything that would bring on the festivities.

Once they finished, they had a few minutes before parents began arriving with picnic items. Emmy gathered her class in the school yard and gave them each a gift.

"Class, I wanted to tell you how proud I am of each of your efforts this year. You have all come a long way." She smiled and felt her lips quiver, but she pressed them together and continued.

"Sam, thank you for being a mature and responsible barn supervisor. Without your assistance, we likely would have lost our barn to an accidental fire," Emmy recalled the unfortunate incident in the dead of winter when Frank Hamm brought a candle to untie his horse from the barn and dropped it on a tinder-dry hay bale. Without Sam's quick action to stomp out the flame, the barn, horses and children could have been in grave danger.

She presented him with a hand-written card and a peppermint candy stick.

"Thank you, Miss Bennett," he said as he ducked his head and accepted the gift.

Emmy repeated the ceremony with each child, remembering a specific good deed or responsible act. The students waited patiently until they each had their candy stick. Then, she released them to enjoy their sweet and have free time in the school yard before the picnic.

At 11:30, parents arrived with salads, sandwiches, cakes and cookies. Emmy and Mel's classes had prepared tables in the school room to lay out the food, tea and lemonade. The children ran in and out of the school, announcing what had arrived. Emmy knew it was pointless to try to reign in their enthusiasm. Instead, she made sure none of the children touched the food until everything was ready.

"We've got ourselves a real nice day for the picnic," Mary said to Emmy after turning another hopeful child away from the goodies.

"Couldn't ask for better," Emmy smiled.

Mr. Purdy strode toward the two women at the food table and Mary exchanged a glance with her friend.

"Hello Miss Bennett," Mr. Purdy said with a shallow bow. "Your classroom looks spic and span."

"Thank you," she replied.

"I would like the chance to speak to you at the end of the day," he continued. "May I drive you home?"

Emmy felt a flash of annoyance. "Thank you, but I was going to ride home with the Drummonds." She pleaded to Mary with her eyes.

"We can excuse you," her friend said with a twinkle in her eye.

Emmy pursed her lips together. "Thank you, Mr. Purdy." She accepted his offer and he scurried away as if to avoid the changing of her mind.

Mary chuckled. "You'll have to tell him," she whispered. "He doesn't seem to take the hint."

More mothers arrived with food before Emmy could respond.

Emmy rang the school bell so Mr. Hamm could take a class photo. Emmy and the other teachers organized the students into rows based on grade, much as they'd been organized in the school. Several of the boys held sticks from the school yard, but she didn't have time to make them put the sticks away with all the parents clambering for a peek. Sam wouldn't take off his cap, but Emmy ignored the problem, smoothed down her navy sailor-striped white dress and patted her hair, hoping it was in place. She didn't realize until the photo had been taken that she still held the school bell.

After the photo, Mr. Purdy said a long, reedy prayer over the food.

"Great, merciful Father in heaven above. We thank you for thy great bounty, Thy care and provisions. . ." and so it went on for several minutes until at last he sighed "Amen". The children raced one another to the banquet table and Emmy hoped the parents knew they had not behaved with such wildness in her classroom. Watching some of the parents elbow themselves to the head of the line, she shrugged and felt she'd done her best.

Cassie hung back with Emmy. "Go ahead, Cassie," Emmy said. "You might miss the cookies."

Cassie sighed and looked at her with wide eyes. "Being with you is more important." She clasped Emmy's hand. Emmy held on tight.

Emmy selected egg salad sandwiches, pickles, Jell-O salad and Mrs. Drummond's scones for lunch. She added lemon juice to her and Cassie's tea and they settled onto the grass near the Drummonds. Several of the boys had already finished their meals and were up practicing the three-legged race. She and Cassie watched and discussed who the winner might be.

"Would you be my partner?" Cassie asked when they had finished their lunch.

Emmy shook her head. "I'm afraid that wouldn't be fair. There are no adults allowed in the children's races.

Cassie snorted with annoyance. "My big brother is taller that you. It isn't fair that I have to race against him." She glared at Sam, but then recovered her good nature and scurried away to ask one of the girls to be her partner.

"Could you ring that bell for us again, Miss Bennett?" said Mr. Hamm a moment later. "Seems you're the only one they'll listen to."

Emmy obliged, and children and adults gathered around.

"Please be seated," Mr. Hamm's voice boomed into the mild spring day. "Before we start the festivities, we need to take a few minutes to honour the graduates and their teacher."

Patsy Hamm and Sam Blaine were among ten students who had passed their grade 8 exams and would be graduating from the elementary school house. Patsy would continue her high school studies by boarding with family members in Shelby. It was they who had recommended Emmy take the school in Harding. Sam's schooling would end today. Emmy had tried to persuade Mrs. Blaine to let him continue his studies. She had even said he could stay with her parents in Shelby, but Mrs. Blaine would not be convinced.

"Grade 8 is more than his father or I ever had. It's good enough for him. We need him working now."

Emmy held her tongue, though she couldn't help thinking that a little more education might have kept Mr. Blaine from risking everyone's life for a Christmas concert.

The graduating grade 8 students received their Certificates of Promotion from the Province of Saskatchewan. They were printed on thick, quality paper and had been signed by Mr. Temple. The girls received a bouquet of flowers while the boys accepted a ball point pen.

Then the younger grades received their certificates of promotion, which were smaller and signed by their teachers, who shook their hands, proud of what they'd accomplished.

Mary Drummond stood to address friends, neighbours and students. "We have been very fortunate to have our teachers, Miss Bennett, Miss Flemming, Miss Lafferty and Miss Fell, this school year. They brought a lot of energy, steady persistence and excellent classroom skills to our community.

"I'm sure we won't soon forget the creative concerts Miss Bennett directed. All our children benefited under her care and instruction. They are more confident, contained and independent for her tutelage. On behalf of the Harding School District, I would like to present her with this small token of our appreciation."

Mary formally shook Emmy's hand. She presented gifts and kind words to the other teachers as well. Then they posed for a photo with the rest of the school board before Mary hugged Emmy and whispered in her ear, "I wish it was more." Emmy took the bouquet of flowers, the envelope and a wrapped present while her students gathered around.

"Please, Miss Bennett. Can't you open it?" several children pleaded.

They crowded around Emmy as she sat on Mary's picnic blanket. The envelope contained a card hand painted by Dahlia Purdy. It was the school house surrounded by spring flowers.

"Dahlia, this is lovely," she exclaimed and hugged the shy girl who blushed.

Inside, the card was filled with the signatures of the students and the school board.

"We had to do it when you weren't looking," Arthur Drummond blurted. "It was hard work!" The adults chuckled.

There was also $25, which would help Emmy get home on the bus. "Thank you," she smiled at the assembled crowd, but felt self-conscious to be receiving money in front of everyone.

"Wow, that's a lot of money, Miss Bennett!" said Cassie. "What will you do with it all?"

"Save it until I need it," Emmy replied. "That's always the best way to manage money."

Finally, she opened the wrapped gift and found a writing set including a ballpoint pen like Sam's, creamy paper, envelopes and stamps.

"So you can write to us," said Florence Drummond.

"It's perfect," Emmy said.

"Let the games begin!" shouted Mr. Hamm once Emmy had wished her students well.

Mr. Hamm started with foot races. First the boys raced and then the girls. Emmy thought Florence Drummond could beat any of the boys, but there was no way to know for sure. Sam took first place for the boys and Florence for the girls. Next were sack races and then the three-legged race. Cassie took second place with her partner, Rosemond Purdy. They were the smallest girls but well-matched in their strides and quickness. Only Sam and Timothy outpaced them. Then, the baseball game began. Younger children were invited to skip or play hopscotch, but soon everyone gathered to see if there would be a home run.

Most of the women sat on the sidelines to mind children or watch the game, but Mary Drummond was a baseball fanatic.

"You'll play, won't you Miss Bennett?" Mary asked.

"Certainly! She was happy to play and Patsy and Florence joined as well. They were sent outfield, but they still got to hit and that was where Mary shone.

"Hit 'er long!" the crowd cheered when she came up to bat. She gathered all the power of her small stocky frame and after two balls, she struck with such force that the baseball flew well outside the field. Emmy cheered.

Mary's team won, and by default, Emmy. It was a thrill she wouldn't forget.

Mary swung an arm around Emmy's shoulder. "Thanks for helping," she said with rosy cheeks and dusty hair. "I'm usually out there alone with all those men. I don't think I've ever been prouder of my Florence." Florence had also fared well on the field and sent two men home on her last hit.

Mr. Hamm gathered the men for the final event of the day: The Tug of War. Mary didn't move to join this event. "Gotta leave them some place to show off," she whispered to Emmy.

Mr. Hamm and Mr. Drummond took turns picking men for their teams. Then they unrolled the long thick rope and used a piece of chalk to draw a midline. They were evenly matched, and Emmy overheard a few choice words exchanged as the men grew red with exertion. She noticed Mr. Purdy did not join and was inching his way closer. Emmy's spirits sank.

"Good afternoon, Miss Bennett," he said when he reached her elbow.

Emmy longed to move away, but she held her place. "Your Rosemond did very well in the three-legged race," she said.

"Thank you," he replied. "Although I prefer my daughters participate in more lady-like activities. She's still young."

Emmy fought a grimace. "Dahlia painted me a

lovely going away card," she said. "It will be nice to have such a pretty keepsake from my first year."

"Perhaps you won't need a keepsake," he said and she felt his eyes piercing her, but she refused to meet his gaze.

The shouting from the Tug-of-war became too loud for conversation and Emmy moved closer to Mrs. Drummond.

Mr. Hamm's team won the fight and suddenly, her first year at Harding School was over. Students and parents said their final goodbyes. Emmy couldn't help shedding a few tears, especially when she shook the hand of Sam Blaine for the last time.

"We'll see you at home," Mrs. Drummond squeezed her arm as the school yard emptied. Emmy felt a flutter of panic, but she forced it down and completed the rest of her duties.

"Where are the girls?" Emmy said after gathering her bag and locking the school door. Mr. Purdy was waiting for her with his horse and buggy at the school steps.

"The Fleishmans took them home." He held out his hand to help her into the buggy.

The buggy was clean and he placed a fur rug on her lap. The horse was groomed and well-fed and Mr. Purdy was still neat after his day at the picnic. He smiled at her and she blushed against her will.

They sat in silence while he guided the horse along the road. Emmy gazed upon the dry and sickly fields that stretched on forever. Why could she not love a man like Mr. Purdy? He had nice daughters and seemed peaceable and kind. She peered at him from the corner of her eye, not wishing to encourage him, but it was too late. He seemed bolstered to speak.

"I am well-aware of your admirable attention to Harding School this year," he said.

Emmy held on to some hope that his was merely a friendly offer to thank her for her work.

"I was there when you signed the agreement not to become married or engaged during your contract," he said and Emmy's heart sank.

"I can only commend your efforts in this area. You don't know how many teachers we've lost part way through the year when they broke this promise." He shook his head and frowned.

"It speaks to your character and I can't tell you how refreshing it is to find a young woman with your impeccable manners and upbringing." He smiled, reminding her of a certain puppy she had as a girl.

"Thank you," she said. "I. . ."

"As you know, I lost my wife four years ago." He turned away from her toward the withered fields. "I've done my best to provide for our girls and teach them everything they need to know, but they're coming upon an age when they need a mother. . ." he let his sentence fade into the early evening.

"You have wonderful daughters. I'm sure many of the women in Harding will be happy to help." She hoped she sounded both gentle and dismissive.

He turned his eyes from the wide-open sky toward her. "I'm ready for another wife," he said, his gaze intense. "I want you. Will you be my wife,

Miss Bennett? Emmy?" His voice held such hope she cringed.

"I'm sorry, Mr. Purdy," she began. His hopeful eyes squinted. "I have great respect for you and a genuine affection for your girls."

He perked up again. "That is certainly more than enough to start," he said. "I have every confidence that is all one needs for a good marriage."

Emmy squeezed her hands on her lap, searching for the right words. "It's not enough for me," she said. "I am looking for love in marriage and I don't think I will find it with you."

Her words hung like a slap between them and Mr. Purdy's eyes watered. "But. . ." he started. He never finished his thought. He slouched into his seat and angled himself away from her. Fortunately, they were only minutes away from the Drummonds and at last she was free of his hopes and sadness.

"Thank you," Emmy said as she climbed out of the buggy. "I hope you find what you're looking for."

He said nothing in return, but his jaw tightened and he neither dismounted to greet the Drummonds nor sent his greetings via Emmy. He pulled the horses around as soon as was possible and Emmy was grateful to have the little drama behind her.

# CHAPTER TWENTY-FOUR

*Shelby*

"Did you hear, Emmy? The Teachers Federation says teachers aren't to sign contracts for less than $700 a year!" Bev handed Emmy a letter as they sat together on the bus ride home.

Emmy read it rapidly. "This war is making big changes for women. They'll even let married women teach."

"Are you sure you want to go back to Harding?" Bev said.

"Yes," Emmy replied without hesitation. "Starting over again somewhere new would be more work than its worth. Are you having second thoughts?"

Bev sighed. "If I can't get married, I might as well be in the classroom." Emmy patted her hand, hoping to ease some of the distress from her friend's face. Emmy's brothers and Lars had shipped off to Ontario that week. It would be a sad homecoming. As little as Emmy wanted to return to her stepfather's house, she couldn't leave the farm work and the housework to her mother and sisters.

The outline of Shelby came into sight in the setting sun. The two church spires competed like the tower of Babel for closeness to God. To Emmy, it felt like shackles tightening. Without Lars around, the summer would be long.

Bev and Emmy stopped chatting as they drew closer to home. Would their taste of independence seem like only a dream tomorrow? Emmy opened her pocketbook to make sure it still held her paycheque. She clasped the pocketbook shut again. Would her stepfather take it all?

Bev put an arm around her shoulders. "We'll meet at the ladies' society meeting on Saturday. They are sewing "dirty bags" for our troops."

"Yes," Emmy nodded, but her focus was distant. They pulled up to the bus stop in Shelby and Emmy scanned the road for her family's wagon. There was Becky, grown willowy tall, waving at the bus and jumping up and down. Emmy sat up, her eyes widening.

"Who's that?" Bev whispered, taking in the man in uniform at Becky's side.

"Lars," Emmy breathed and her heart began to race.

An interminable amount of time passed before the bus stopped and disgorged its passengers. Emmy hurried to her sister and Lars who stood back to allow the sisters to embrace first.

"Mama said she's sorry she couldn't come, but she thought you wouldn't mind." Becky waggled her eyebrows at Lars and nudged her sister toward him.

"What are you doing here?" Emmy said.

Lars chuckled. "I came all this way for that greeting?" He reached for Emmy and pulled her into an embrace.

Becky clucked her tongue. "What will the neighbours think?" she teased.

Lars let go of Emmy and turned to Becky. "Remember what we talked about?"

Becky saluted Lars and skipped off toward the General store, a bright coin twinkling in her hand.

"You aren't under contract at present, are you?" Lars said, staring deeply into Emmy's eyes.

"No," Emmy's forehead knit together.

Lars dropped to one knee. The other passengers had moved away by that time, so they were alone on the road. Emmy gasped.

"I head out to Petawawa tomorrow morning," he said. "They let me stay behind one more week. I'm not fit for service overseas. Flat feet," he patted his shoes and shrugged.

"Tomorrow," Emmy murmured, tears springing to her eyes.

"I know you planned to stay here and work for the summer. You may still do this, but if you'd like, I can take you with me." His eyes were hopeful.

"To Ontario?" Emmy said. Some part of her understood what was happening, but another part of her needed it spelled out one letter at a time.

"I can only bring you if you are my wife."

"Wife?"

"Emmy Bennett, will you marry me and live with me on the Canadian Army base?" His smile wavered.

"But how can we marry by tomorrow?"

Lars shook his head and laughed. "My Emmy. Always so practical. You can leave all the details to me. I just need to have your answer."

"Yes. Yes, I want to be with you. Wherever you go."

Lars stood and pressed Emmy to his chest. Then he tipped her head toward him and kissed her there for anyone to see. When he pulled away, he said "Hot dog! I'm the luckiest man in the world."

Emmy laughed and tears fell down her cheeks. Becky ran up to them then, with a little box in her hand, a lollipop in the other.

"Corporal Bennett, at your service!" she shouted and saluted once more.

"At ease, corporal," Lars said. Becky giggled and dropped her hand, standing on tiptoes to see what was in the box.

Lars opened thebox, it contained a simple gold band with a garnet stone. "For you, my dear. I love you."

Lars kept one arm around Emmy's shoulders and while the other hand held the reins. Becky kept up a lively one-sided conversation on the way back.

"I'll be the first girl at school with a married sister. Well, there is Kate, but her sister is ancient. And she wasn't born here, so I think I still count as the first. Let me see that ring again, Emmy."

Emmy held out her hand to her sister who traced

the pattern of the stone with her small, warm fingers. "It's so pretty, Emmy. I want one just like it. But not garnet. My birthday's not in January. It'll have to be Ruby."

As they drew near the farmhouse, Emmy's emotions roiled. She'd been so sure. Why was her heart beating so quickly, her mouth so dry and her knees knocking together?

"Why don't you run along inside, Becky. Tell your Ma we need a few minutes to ourselves, but don't say anything yet."

"Mum's the word!" Becky clamped her lips together and floated inside.

"I sprung this on you, Emmy. We haven't seen each other in a couple of months and now I'm rushing you. You can change your mind. I'll understand."

Emmy wanted to say no, but she found she had no voice at all. So unlike her.

Lars pressed her once more to his heart. "I'm going to drop you off here. Do you think you can manage your luggage? It feels so ungentlemanly, but I feel it's what I must do right now."

Emmy nodded and one of the knots inside her stomach loosened an inch. "Thank you, Lars. That's just what I need."

"I'll come back at supper time. It's been arranged with your Mother. If you don't want me to stay, all you have to do shake your head." He bent down to kiss her cheek. "It'll be alright. Either way." He gave one sad smile and turned. She stood in the tall grass and let him drive away.

Her shoulders sagged. What would she say to her family? She bent down to lift her suitcase and hurried inside before she could change her mind.

There was no time to think. She had to reassure her mother she'd been eating enough, entertain her siblings with teaching stories, as well as unpack and freshen up. Then Lars turned up as promised. Emmy answered the door which she'd been watching like a hawk the past half hour.

"Evening. Mind if I come in?" Lars' eyes were so hopeful, she managed a quick smile and ushered him in. Becky rushed to greet him.

"Supper's all ready. We got a haggis, just for you!" she flitted out of the entryway and everyone gathered at the dinner table for prayers and conversation. Plates of food, water and tea were passed. Emmy hardly noticed where it was all coming and going and then her stepfather pounced on Lars.

"Have you given up trapping, then?"

"That's right," Lars said.

"How do you plan to support yourself once this blasted war is through?" He stuffed another piece of haggis in his mouth.

"I can't rightly say, sir. After tonight, I'll head to Petawawa to work in supplies. Who knows what this country will need once the war ends?"

Her stepfather grunted and wiped his mouth on his sleeve. "When I was your age, I had land of my own. Had my whole life planned out. Good thing too, with this darned Depression. I watched a lot of men drift off, riding the rails, living in relief camps. Fools, the lot of them."

Emmy looked to her mother for help, but she was carefully cutting her pickled beans.

"It's been a difficult time, sir. You were lucky you could provide for your family," Lars said.

"Nonsense." Her stepfather rose. "Luck has nothing to do with anything. Jean, I'll take my coffee and pie in the parlour." He stomped away from the table while Emmy's siblings looked after him, her sister Mary shaking her head.

Becky broke the awkward silence. "Lars tell us what you ate when you were trapping. Did you have to bring all your supplies?"

An inviting smile spread across Lars's face. He still had at least half of his food on his plate, but he abandoned his fork and knife and turned his eyes to Becky.

"We brought in as much flour, sugar, molasses, tinned milk and lard as we could manage," he said. "But the rest we had to hunt or scavenge ourselves. Our first year, I was the youngest, so they made me cook."

"Really? My brothers would starve. They can't even boil water!"

Jack pretended to cuff his sister who squealed in protest.

"Mostly, we ate meat," Lars said. "Caribou, deer and moose were plentiful. I'd serve it with a batch of bannock and some stewed dried fruit. But we had a few things to learn from our more experienced neighbours."

"Who were your neighbours?" Becky was entranced.

"The Chipewyan hunters had a camp nearby. We were grateful for their generosity in sharing their food and experience.

"Out in the cold, you start to crave fat and sugar. We were always hungry. Several years in, we met five of these hunters and huddled together in the Cree Lake Outpost. It was so cold we kept the fire burning all the time. We set a large aluminum pot on top of the stove and filled it with huge chunks of frozen meat. Once it was boiled, it was some of the tastiest meat I ever ate.

"We'd fish the meat out of the pot, pick off the hairs and chew it down to the bone."

"Hooey! The meat had hair?" Becky said.

Lars chuckled. "It's a different life up there. We learned the best meat you'll ever eat is moose nose."

"You're giving us an earful," said Howard with a huge grin.

"Not this time." Lars's eyes sparkled. "As long as you prepare it right."

"So how do you prepare a moose nose?" said Becky.

Lars had scooped up a forkful of coleslaw, but he set it back down to gesture with his hands.

"After you cut the nose off the moose, you need a piece of forked willow." He made a fork with two of his fingers. "You slide the nostrils through the fork so you can burn off the hair and skin over the campfire." He mimed the action and then looked to Emmy's mother with a cringe.

"Sorry, Mrs. Young. Is this too much for polite company?"

"Not a whit." Her mother smiled. "You've just eaten our haggis, so you see we don't mind a bit of adventurous cooking."

"Yes ma'am," he smiled. "After the campfire, you peel off the skin, so the nose is about the size and colour of a large coconut." He demonstrated the size with his hands.

"Next, you cut the meat into chocolate bar-sized pieces and boil it for two and one-half hours. Then, it's ready to eat."

"What's it taste like?" said Howard, his face a bit white.

"It's nice, like fat pork with a hint of birch and willow, jack pine tips and water lilies. All the things a moose likes to eat."

"I would never have imagined such a thing," said Emmy's mother, rising from her chair. "Girls, help me clear away the supper things so we can have dessert."

Emmy's mother put a heavy hand on her shoulder to signal she was to remain seated with the men and boys.

"Bev says hello," Emmy said with a special eye on her brother. "She hopes to see us at the Christmas Eve service."

"How did Bev like her class?" Emmy's mother asked.

"Very well," Emmy said and continued for her brother's sake. "They were quite taken with her. I think she could ask them to scrape gum off the ceiling and they'd only beam at her. They come to school early so they can be the first to bring her an apple." Emmy laughed. "We've been making applesauce, apple cake and apple pie all year."

Lars finally had time to finish his supper as the dishes were cleared. When Becky came to his elbow, he handed her his plate. "What part of the meal did you make?" he said.

Becky sighed. "Mother would only let me help her. She says I'm too much of a dunderheid to make things on my own yet."

"Becky!" her mother said, cheeks colouring.

Lars laughed. "Does she now?" Becky took his empty plate and placed it precariously on the counter. Her mother grasped it before it had a chance to crash to the floor.

"Well, my girl, now you go and give him an example."

Emmy's brothers laughed, but Emmy stood to hug her little sister. "Don't mind them," she said. "Lord knows what would happen if they ever helped in the kitchen."

Emmy's mother placed the first plate of mincemeat pie in her hands. "Now that you're up, could you take that to Dad?" she said.

Emmy flinched, but closed her eyes a minute and nodded. "Of course." She left the warm kitchen for the dark parlour. Her stepfather glowered from his faded upholstered armchair. The stuffing poked out of several places. His eyes were closed when she entered but opened to survey her progress.

"Here you are, father," she said and placed the

rose-patterned dessert plate and a fork in his hand. He took a huge mouthful of pie and grunted. Emmy turned to leave the room.

"Is your young man going to take you off our hands, then?"

Emmy stopped and peered at him. "Is that what you'd like?"

"One less mouth to feed." He took another forkful of pie. "But don't expect to come crying home to us when he can't provide for you. Once you're married, you're his responsibility."

"I don't need anyone taking care of me," she said, her voice low but strong. "I can earn my own way now. I'm a professional teacher."

Her stepfather grunted, shovelled the last bit of pie into his mouth and held the plate out to Emmy. "That money you earned belongs to your family," he said. Emmy's hand shook as she took the plate and she nearly broke it when she slammed it onto the kitchen counter. Emmy's mother's eyes widened, but no one else seemed to notice.

Emmy found it difficult to follow any of the conversation for the rest of the evening. "I said, Emmy, could you pass the cream?" Jim enunciated as she fiddled with her pie.

She gazed at Lars from time to time until he caught her glance and gave her a look of concern. But there was no more time to talk privately as they cleared the dessert dishes.

After supper, her mother shooed everyone out of doors except Emmy. They began a batch of cookies.

Emmy measured the flour, oatmeal and sugar when her mother drew her into the safety of the coatroom.

"Your stepfather thinks you're marrying Lars." Her eyes searched Emmy's.

Emmy stiffened and stared at her house shoes. Had he poisoned her mother against her?

"We can't get married unless I give up teaching," Emmy said without looking at her mother's face.

Suddenly her mother pulled her into her strong arms. Emmy gazed at her face and saw her eyes were glistening and she was smiling. "He's a wonderful man. I know you'll be happy together."

It took Emmy several breaths to reply. "Thank you, Mother."

"What are your plans?" she said after she released Emmy.

Suddenly Emmy saw her path clearly. "I'll work one more year in Harding and meet him in Ontario once he's settled. We'll have a civil service. I'm sorry, Mother. . ."

Her mother batted away her apology. "It's for the best. Who can afford a wedding nowadays? I'll make you a dress."

Emmy covered her mouth with her hand. "Thank you, Mum." She bit her lip and her shoulders slumped.

"What is it, dear?" her mother touched Emmy's arm.

Emmy shook her head, she couldn't ask, yet her mother read her thoughts.

"Your stepfather was handsome and strong." Her mother's words were barely audible. "We'd lived with my sister for three years. With all her children and more on the way, she was in a hurry to be rid of us. He didn't drink yet. . ."

Emmy found her nerve. "Is there any way to tell if Lars will become a drinker?"

Her mother pursed her lips until they nearly disappeared. "Your stepfather lost his mother before he could even remember her. He knows how to provide for his family, but not to love. He's been a good provider.

"Lars loves you." She squeezed her daughter once more and brushed her cheek with a feathery kiss. Then, she straightened her apron and returned to the kitchen.

# CHAPTER TWENTY-FIVE

---

*All's Fair*

*One Year later*

Emmy worried over her hair. The miles seemed to be slipping by too slowly, and each time she checked her pocket mirror, another hair was trying to escape her carefully curled style. Emmy fingered one of the oversized buttons which decorated the front of the dress. Her mother had found the latest style and hand-embroidered the flowers on the breast.

"If I can't be there to give you flowers, I will sew them on myself." Her mother's lined face wore a brave smile despite the tears hiding in her eyelashes.

The landscape changed dramatically once they left Manitoba. Emmy thought of the lessons she'd given on Canadian geography comparing the Prairie to the Canadian Shield. She'd never seen it for herself. The movement from grasses to rock felt desolate. Would she ever again be home?

It was night when she arrived at the station in Petawawa. She had enough money. She could get off the train, buy another ticket and return to what she knew. But when she looked out the window, she saw her tall, handsome soldier, in a freshly pressed suit with shining buttons and a dark, neatly knotted tie. He carried the largest corsage she'd ever seen. His eyes were so earnest, she checked her fears, smiled and waved from her window. His hopeful eyes filled with mirth.

"You've come," he said enveloping Emmy, her suitcase and her purse into one massive hug. She could hardly breathe. It was the best feeling in the world.

"You look dynamite," he tilted up her chin and dipped her low to kiss her full on the lips. Emmy heard someone give an appreciative whistle. When he stood her up again, she patted her hair.

"Pardon me," Lars said. He took her bags in one hand and wrapped his other arm around her waist. "Your chariot awaits." She nearly had to run to keep up to him as he ushered her to a cream coloured Oldsmobile.

"Yours?" she asked, breathless, once they were seated.

Lars chuckled. "I wish! Our squad leader lends out his car for weddings. It's his gift. I need to have it back by tomorrow night."

Emmy heard a giggle from the back seat and turned to find another soldier with his arm around a pretty blond woman wearing a pink dress. Even in the dark, Emmy could see the woman's lipstick was smudged and seemed to have traveled to the soldier's lips.

"This is my friend Rick and his wife, Vera. They're going to be our witnesses."

Emmy shook their hands.

"It'll be so good to have another woman on the base!" Vera said. "Now there are six of us."

"Only six?" Emmy said.

"Does that worry you, sweetheart?" Rick teased.

Emmy found herself in her response. "Not a bit. I have 5 brothers. It'll be just like home."

Rick chuckled and Vera squealed.

"We're almost there," Lars said from the driver's seat. "Are you ready?"

"Yes," Emmy said, clutching the corsage he'd placed in her hands.

"Wait here," Lars said after he parked the car. Emmy obliged while Lars circled the car to hold the door open for her.

When she stepped out, she noticed a couple with their heads titled toward one another at the stairs to a cobblestone building. Emmy recognized their profiles instantly.

"Howard! Bev!" She was holding Lars' hand, but he squeezed it once and let go so she could run to her brother and sister-in-law.

She embraced them together, tears rushing to her eyes. Bev kissed her cheek and put a hand on either shoulder and gently pushed her away and pulled out a handkerchief.

"There, there, Emmy. This won't do. You've made Lars wait a whole year. You can't get married with tears." She wiped Emmy's face and then tutted at the corsage which was looking a bit limp in Emmy's hands.

"Come inside. I'll pin this on in the light. Did you know, I heard they are starting to let married women teach? Maybe this won't be the end of your career after all. Now chin up!"

Emmy felt her spirits soar at the news. It had been so difficult to leave her class at the end of term. Some of the sadness weighing on her heart dissipated and she was able to turn her focus to the little group crowding into the office where they would be married. Emmy tried to catch up on all the news in the few minutes they had before the ceremony.

"Why are you back, Howie?" she started with her brother.

"An injury," he said with a bright smile, but a darkness in his eyes Emmy had never seen before. "I haven't told mother yet, but I couldn't miss my favourite sister's wedding."

"We'll come to Petawawa in a month, Emmy. Howard will work with Lars on the base. We can all be together again!"

"That's wonderful!" Emmy couldn't make her words match her emotions. She felt wooden with shock. She hadn't seen her brother in a year and to have him back just at the right moment was inconceivable.

Lars turned up at her side. "They're ready for us Emmy."

She turned to face him and smiled. He'd waited

for her while she continued teaching and made sure she wanted to marry. Even when Bev left to move to Ontario to marry Howard a week before he was shipped overseas. Emmy couldn't leave her classroom, but Lars had kept writing and visited at Christmas. They'd only had two days together all year, but he'd proven steady calm and sober despite the army's reputation for drink and revelry.

"This is perfect, Lars." She said, taking his arm and kissing his cheek. "Thank you."

He grinned broadly and they listened together to the words that would set them up for a lifetime together. Emmy was sure at last.

# A LOOK AT AFTER HIS HEART:

Women can't resist David King. David has been chosen by Saul, the head pastor of a mega church in California to lead worship, but now Saul seems to have turned his back on his protégé. Saul's daughter, Michaela, can't figure out what has changed. Eventually, Michaela is swayed by her father's wishes and allows herself to be wooed by another man. Saul fires David and he is left friendless, penniless and jobless.

Abigail and her husband Kurt Nabal have a lucrative record label. When Abigail meets David, he has nothing. She is amazed by his burgeoning talent and when her husband tries to take advantage of David, she steps in to make a real offer.

Years later, Beth's husband is fighting in Iraq while she awaits his return. While enjoying a late-night swim, David suddenly appears at her door. She ignores all of her mores and beliefs to be with him for one night. What will their infidelity cost?

*AVAILABLE ON AMAZON NOW!*

# ABOUT THE AUTHOR

Samantha Adkins grew up in the Rocky Mountains of Canada. Following in the footsteps of her father and grandfather, she is a born story-teller. She studied journalism and professional writing at Mount Royal College in Alberta. She enjoys reading and writing in a variety of genres. Her writing is inspired by the works of Jane Austen, Lemony Snicket (aka Daniel Handler), Judy Blume, Louise Penny, Roald Dahl, Bodie Thoene, and Lois Lowry.

Samantha enjoys imagining well-known stories in different settings. Expectations, Suspiciously Reserved, and Banff Springs Abbey are inspired by Jane Austen's novels. After His Heart and Not As They Appear imagine classic Biblical tales in modern settings.

Living on a small island off the West Coast of Canada, Samantha Adkins loves spending time at the ocean with her two children, teaching elementary school, and walking the rocky trails with her husband and friends. Reading and writing are the perfect pastimes for the long, rainy winter months.